OLDUVAI

Steve Bull

ISBN
978-1-4602-0690-4 (Hardcover)
978-1-4602-0689-8 (Paperback)
978-1-4602-0691-1 (eBook)

Produced by:

FriesenPress

Suite 300 – 852 Fort Street
Victoria, BC, Canada V8W 1H8

www.friesenpress.com

Distributed to the trade by The Ingram Book Company

For my family.

However much we like to think of ourselves as something special in world history, in fact industrial societies are subject to the same principles that caused earlier societies to collapse. If civilization collapses again, it will be from failure to take advantage of the current reprieve, a reprieve both detrimental and essential to our anticipated future.

Joseph Tainter, 1988
The Collapse of Complex Societies

Those past collapses tended to follow somewhat similar courses constituting variations on a theme. Population growth forced people to adopt intensified means of agricultural production…Unsustainable practices led to environmental damage…Consequences for society included food shortages, starvation, wars among too many people fighting for too few resources, and overthrows of governing elites by disillusioned masses. Eventually, population decreased through starvation, war, or disease and society lost some of the political, economic, and cultural complexity that it had developed at its peak.

Jared Diamond, 2005
Collapse: How Societies Choose to Fail or Succeed

Since the 1950s, the Olduvai Gorge in Tanzania has been strongly associated with human origins and the Stone-age way-of-life. In this discussion the 'Olduvai Theory' is a metaphor. It suggests our impending return to a Stone-age way-of-life.

Richard C. Duncan, 1996
The Olduvai Theory: Sliding Towards a Post-Industrial Stone Age

Delays in feedback loops are critical determinants of system behavior. They are common causes of oscillations...a system just can't respond to short-term changes when it has long-term delays...

A delay in a feedback process is critical relative to rates of change in the stocks that the feedback loop is trying to control. Delays that are too short cause overreaction, 'chasing your tail,' oscillations amplified by the jumpiness of the response. Delays that are too long cause damped, sustained or exploding oscillations, depending on how much too long. Overlong delays in a system with a threshold, a danger point, a range past which irreversible damage can occur, cause overshoot and collapse.

Donella H. Meadows, 2008
Thinking in Systems: A Primer

April 3, 6:30 a.m.

Dave clambered over another group of fallen trees as he wound his way down towards the river that cut through the forest he was traversing. The sheen of a late spring frost could be seen just ahead. It was one of the few spots in this dense group of trees where early morning sunshine would be able to penetrate to the forest floor. The sunlight reflected off some crystallised ice on a few dead leaves clustered together against a tree trunk near the river's edge.

Amongst the constantly shifting shadows and between the patches of snow that had been fighting to keep from melting into the surrounding deadwood and decaying leaves, a few dozen trilliums were fighting to shake off their winter sleep. The plants could be seen just poking their heads through the wet leaves and soil, seeking some early morning warmth.

A gust of wind blew around a few of the leaves and up into Dave's face, leaving a touch of dirt on his nose and cheek. He wiped at his face but only managed to smudge the dirt across his cheek, giving him a dark streak similar to those worn by some athletes when playing field sports.

It was time to pause for a moment's rest as his back was beginning to feel the effect of sleeping on the semi-frozen ground for the past three nights. Last evening was probably the least comfortable. As the sunlight was beginning to wane he had found a patch of dense forest and curled up behind a wall of thick cedars and underbrush but more importantly out of the chilling, northwesterly wind blowing down off Lake Huron.

Thankfully the wind had not picked up until later in the afternoon. He had been able to spend most of the day in bright, warm sunshine as he shuffled north on another gravel road. For three days Dave had been making his way northeast, using roads most of the way but occasionally cutting through forests and across abandoned fields.

Every few hours he pulled a compass out of his knapsack to ensure he was more or less on the right track, cross-checking the map he had found amongst his gear with local features. What he wouldn't give for a GPS unit, he thought. This was overly optimistic thinking, however, as both satellite and cellular communication had been down for at least a couple of months.

He would not have to go through all this if he would just stick to the roads, but Dave seldom took the easiest path. He had figured that the timing would be pretty similar, about four or five days, so being somewhat more adventurous and needing to practise some old skills he chose to cut across large areas of land with no obvious roads or other significant landmarks.

He could feel the sun on his face as he glanced up through the leafless, hardwood trees. The days were getting warmer and he half-hoped today would be another unseasonably warm, spring day like most of yesterday.

Dave felt physically fine apart from the stiff back. His mind, however, continued to be haunted by the situation he found himself in. He still could not believe that everything had fallen apart so quickly. One day he was planning his next trip south for some golf and not seventeen months later he found himself walking through an abandoned countryside on his way to his older brother's home instead of getting on a plane and heading to South Carolina for a few rounds of early, spring golf.

Or was it quick, he reflected. Dave's brother, Sam, had been suggesting for years that this kind of event was likely to happen. The words of his brother during their last conversation still echoed through his head. "It is only a matter of time and if things are looking desperate, I'll likely head north. You know you're welcome to join me."

So here he was, trekking northeast between abandoned small towns trying not to think of what was happening everywhere else in the province. But as Sam reminded him continually, it only takes a single snowflake to cause a devastating avalanche, and it's random as to which snowflake and when a slide will start. He still recalled with vividness that first conversation with his older brother about avalanches...

"So, when is an avalanche triggered?" Sam asked his younger brother somewhat rhetorically.

"What?" Dave asked, off guard given the question he'd just posed. "I suppose it's a combination of too much snow, current weather conditions, temper-"

"Okay, stop for a minute," Sam interrupted. "You're naming all the elements involved. What actually caused the avalanche to begin at the moment it did? What was particular about that moment in time? What triggered the avalanche?" Sam asked trying to steer his brother's thinking towards a different perspective.

"I'm not sure what you're asking me," Dave answered after a moment's pause.

"Okay, let me see if I can think of a better example," Sam offered, pausing for a moment as well. "Do you remember the scene from the first *Jurassic Park* movie when Jeff Goldblum's character is trying to explain Chaos Theory to Laura Dern's character?" Sam eventually asked, knowing his younger brother's addiction to watching movies.

"Sure," Dave answered quickly. He was a huge Michael Crichton fan so he had seen the *Jurassic Park* trilogy several times.

"So, Goldblum drops water onto the back of Dern's hand several times in a row showing how each time the path of the water is different and will continue to follow this unpredictable pattern due to the incalculable variables involved, from the variations in her skin cells to properties of the hairs on the back of her hand," Sam continued.

"Yes, I remember. Goldblum's character is basically talking about the unpredictability of complex systems," Dave responded.

"Good, you've still got a hold of the rope. Now stay with me," Sam quipped. "Instead of an avalanche, think of a pile of sand and placing a single grain of sand on the top of the pile every few seconds. What's going to happen after a while?"

"There will be a slide of sand."

"Why at a particular moment?" Sam probed.

"Well, because the weight will be too much for the underlying grains to support and the accumulating mass of sand will overcome the forces of friction and whoosh."

"You're getting warm," Sam said in a congratulatory tone. "So, if we repeat the experiment dozens or hundreds of times, do you think a major slide will occur at about the same time, if all other conditions are the same?"

"It should, all other things being equal," Dave replied, but not entirely sure now.

"Well, in fact, experiments examining this found that there is no predictability as to how and when a major slide will occur. A major slide could occur quickly after the beginning of the experiment, when few grains of sand had been added; or, a slide could take a relatively long time to occur and require much more sand. Does that make sense to you?"

"Not really," Dave answered after a moment's silence. "You'd think there'd be some consistency."

"So, think about the fact that there is no consistency, no formula for calculating when a slide will occur. What appears to happen is that each grain of sand interacts with those immediately adjacent to it. An interacting group of grains can be in something called a critical state or phase transition, I can't remember verbatim. Anyways, this is a state that with only one more grain of sand those particular grains can overcome friction and begin to slide.

"As a slide begins the moving grains interact with stationary grains. These other grains may not be anywhere near a critical state and end up stalling the slide; or, they could also be close to a critical state and add their mass and energy to the slide."

"Your point?" Dave responded bluntly as he was getting a bit frustrated by his brother's long-winded answer; he just wanted to get back to watching the Canadian Open. "I asked you when you thought this **collapse** could happen!"

"I'm trying to teach you why your question doesn't have an answer," Sam explained. "Just be patient and remember this point because it's really important to understand."

"It's just," Dave started, then paused not wanting to hurt his older brother's feelings. "It's just that you're starting to sound like my teachers."

"Well, I just hope they taught you some critical thinking skills because you might need them to be able to understand life outside of sports. Anyways, critical states or phase transitions, what are they?" Sam continued.

Dave paused for a moment then responded to his brother's question. "It's the point when a group of sand grains are ready to overcome friction with the addition of one more grain. I guess we could think about it as the time between transitioning from one phase, say stasis, to another phase, say movement. Am I close enough, Einstein?" he asked, motioning towards the television that was on in front of him.

"Close enough," Sam ceded but he wasn't going to let his brother off that easy—his lesson wasn't finished, so he continued. "The interesting thing about this research was that no matter how many times the experiment was carried out, no predictable pattern emerged that could be used to predict when or how a massive slide would occur, there were far too many variables involved."

"Okay, I see," Dave started, beginning to grasp his brother's point. "There are too many variables involved in trying to predict when the world is going to collapse."

"I didn't say the world was going to collapse. I said that we could see a devastating series of events cascade through our globally-interconnected systems to cause a major catastrophe."

"I'm sorry, was that English?" Dave snickered. "You're killing me here, Sam."

"Sorry," Sam replied a bit sheepishly. He forgot sometimes that his brother was still in high school and more interested in sports and girls than reading. "Okay, let me try again. Our critical systems, like finance, trade, and energy, all depend on each other. And these systems rely on similar systems worldwide. That's our current state of affairs on a global scale, and I know you know about positive and negative feedback loops. Well, these feedback loops are riddled throughout all these systems and their subsystems."

"Yes, like a thermostat, I remember that conversation well," Dave added and pretended to nod off.

Sam ignored his brother's antics and continued, "Yes, a thermostat is a good example of a simple system; one without many variables involved, however. Think for a moment about all the systems around the globe and how fragile some of them are: oil supplies, for example.

"So, if we have many systems in a fragile or critical state, ready to transition from stable to unstable, when might a catastrophe or an avalanche happen?" Sam asked, his body language suggesting that

Dave should now get that light bulb going off over his head, indicating he understood.

"You can't tell. I understand now," Dave responded proudly.

"Good. I can't tell you when this transition might happen. I can only tell you that I believe we are getting closer to that point. I can confidently argue that some results are more likely than others but no one outcome is guaranteed. There are surprises everywhere and as far as when, anyone who claims to be able to predict the future is mad. Or an economist," Sam added.

...Dave used to get so frustrated with these lessons from his brother. He did, however, have to admit that he had learned an awful lot during them. It was all in the way Sam asked questions; it made Dave have to come to the correct answer himself. He had to really think about what was being asked and where Sam was leading him. It was so tortuous at times though, especially when he was younger and just wanted to play or watch sports. No, maybe it was tortuous all the time he thought, and smiled thinking fondly of his older brother. Smart guy but no—he searched for the words—no social skills, especially around women.

A quick rinse of his face and he would be ready to move on. Despite the warming weather, the water was extremely cold. His hands tingled almost to the point of being painful as he dipped them into the water and splashed his face to help shake off the sleep. His mind flashed back to a canoe trip as a youngster and washing in clean river water for the first time. Since that day Dave had found washing in spring-fed river water better than coffee to shake off a night's sleep. He hadn't canoed in years, however, and he had to remind himself where he was.

This was no spring-fed river in northern Ontario. He knew that this water was not nearly as clean as those he had canoed in years ago. Even the ones he used to ply with a paddle were no longer as clean as they used to be. Being close to farmland would ensure that there would be fossil fuel-based pesticides, herbicides, and fertilisers, not to mention other waste by-products, in the local water. His small filtration unit could filter most of these toxins out but if he could go without, he would. He only rinsed his face this morning as he still had enough clean water in his pack to last another day or two. In fact, he could stretch out his clean water supply almost indefinitely, if he was forced to.

He brought up another handful of water and rubbed his face somewhat vigourously. He had not had a restful sleep these past three nights. It wasn't so much the cold as Dave had learned as a child how to survive in the wilderness regardless of weather conditions. It was the unfolding of world events over the past few years and months that haunted his thoughts, making it difficult to sleep.

When he did sleep, his dreams were filled with morphed, post-apocalyptic scenes reminiscent of the movies *The Book of Eli* and the *Resident Evil* series. Social chaos loomed heavy in every aspect of his dreams during his fitful REM sleep. No vampires, zombies, or mechanical terminators entered his dreams, only a few abandoned children looking for their parents. They had lost their way during this nightmarish clash among people just trying to survive another day. It wasn't all bad, he thought in retrospect. Milla Jovovich and Kate Beckinsale had been there to help him.

Dave opened his pack to retrieve his canteen, a birthday present from his brother along with everything else in the knapsack he now found himself carrying through some woodlot in the middle of southwestern Ontario.

Sam had 'stolen' Dave's pack during a visit last year and then returned it to him full of survival gear on his last birthday...

Dave looked at his older brother with a puzzled grin after opening the large gift bag Sam had surrendered to him when he had arrived for a birthday visit. "When did you take this?" he asked with amusement.

"Last time I was here. It was sitting in the corner of your front closet and I thought I'd fill it with some goodies for your birthday."

"Thanks, brudda," Dave said, using the nickname he had given his older brother when he was still a toddler. "What goodies might I find?

A few Titleist, Calloway—what is this stuff?" Dave exclaimed as he opened the bag and looked inside.

"Just do your older and much wiser brother a favour, put this back in the corner of the front closet and in an emergency take it with you. You'll find a lot of familiar toys and some new ones. Just keep it safe and always accessible. You never know when a black swan might swoop into town."

"Black swan?" Dave asked, and then regretted it immediately.

"Let me explain," Sam began as he placed an arm around his younger brother's shoulder.

As soon as he had asked the question, Dave knew they weren't going anywhere for his twenty-third birthday without having to be subjected to his brother giving him the abridged version of some philosophical treatise that he'd read about, or scientific model he had been thinking about, or—whatever. He wished his brother would show interest in something other than reading and writing.

Sam suggested they stay in and catch whatever was on CBC. He then proceeded to explain to Dave the idea of a black swan. But, it was over a beer while they watched the Leafs playing the Canadiens, a classic original six game. So there was that, Dave thought, as he tried to tune out his brother during the game.

…Here he was in the middle of a black swan, he thought. Well, no, it wasn't exactly a black swan for him because he had been warned about this possibility. But, for most people this was definitely a black swan; it was an unknown unknown. Everything had seemed relatively normal up until about six months ago.

He opened up the pack a bit wider and looked in. His brother had put a small camp stove and a litre of fuel in the pack, but Dave skipped making tea this morning. He had more than enough fuel to get him to his brother's and wanted to get going as quickly as possible because he knew, deep down inside, that tea every morning was a luxury.

He stood to stretch his back and legs then knelt to pick up his backpack, noticing that its straps were fraying badly. By the end of today, he hoped, he would have no further need for it. Adjusting it firmly across his back, he took his bearings and headed towards the sunrise.

His brother had been preparing for this event for years and Dave knew that he had a greater chance of survival, if he got to his brother's...

"What makes you so sure that the world is going to end?" Dave replied to Sam's latest diatribe.

"I never said the world was going to end. Did you never listen to the debates Susie and I used to have? Or anything I've been saying for the past hour?"

"No, not really, you and Susie have always been way too serious. Besides, there's a Leafs game on and they might actually make the play-offs this year."

"Okay, it's intermission. Turn the TV off and listen to me for three minutes," Sam began. "This isn't about the world ending; it's about being prepared for the unexpected. It's about recognizing that it's the things you don't know about that are the ones that can have the most impact on you."

"What? The things I don't know about? Oh yes the, ah," he paused, taking a moment for his brain to retrieve the memory. "The unknown unknowns as Rumsfeld stated to the press during one of those interviews regarding the US invasion of Iraq, yes?"

"Were you watching that stuff? I thought you'd be watching hockey or golf at that age."

"You and Susie were watching it. I was just there being tortured by the two of you and your constant arguing."

"It was debating. Anyways, the idea of a black swan event comes from earlier times when the term 'as likely as a black swan' arose around the probability of an event being impossible. You see, early Europeans only had experience with white swans and-"

"But there are both black and white swans," Dave interjected as he got up to grab another beer. "Another?" he asked Sam, holding up his bottle.

"Correct, and no thanks," Sam replied. "So, language around event probability evolved without the knowledge of black swans. Europeans had only been exposed to white swans," Sam continued as Dave walked into his adjoining kitchen.

"A black swan event then is when you encounter something outside of your expectations or knowledge," Dave suggested, as the line of thinking his brother had started in him began to come together.

"Yes, so always be prepared," Sam replied in return.

"Be prepared. Yes, I remember the Boy Scout pledge Dad always reminded us about."

"In hindsight, Dad just maybe lucked upon preparing us for what could be coming our way: a massive social collapse on a scale no one alive today has truly witnessed."

"Yeah, yeah, world-ending collapse, I got that part. Listen, seriously, the third period is about to start and there's still no score. You've got about one minute left," Dave informed Sam.

"Well, you understand what a black swan event is now, right?"

"I think so; it's about encountering things outside our, what would Dad call it? Paradigm, right? Experience, models-of-the-world kinda stuff."

"Yes, but what about if your model of the world includes realistic possibilities that others don't have?"

"So, my worldview differs from others—then, I guess a certain event might not be a black swan to me. It would be a black swan, however, to the person whose model of the world didn't include that event."

"Exactly. For some, it might be being prepared for a collapse of, say, ah, the fiat currency system," Sam suggested, struggling for a moment to think of something that might appeal to Dave's senses.

"So, I buy gold and silver as a hedge against inflation. In the meantime, the fiat currency system collapses and I'm **golden** because humans have trusted gold and silver as a type of wealth for thousands of years. It can't be printed out of thin air by the elite like paper money," Dave said giving his brother two thumbs up and a big grin.

"More or less, yes," Sam responded as he rolled his eyes. "The pack is a survival kit in case of an emergency. It's an insurance policy, that's all."

"Thanks, brudda. Good timing too as the third period is starting," said Dave, as he took another sip of his beer and returned his focus to the television.

… As he reached the top of a rolling hill Dave caught a brief scent of smoke. His mind quickly entered survival mode; wildfire was his first thought. How far back to the river and was it big enough to act as a natural break? He quickly scanned the area. It had obviously been clear-cut some years ago for although the forest was relatively thick, it was made up of a single species of tree, all about the same age. Apart from the few dense patches of cedars he had encountered, there was little else.

He noted the direction of the wind, estimated the distance back to the river, and scanned the area to determine the amount of combustible underbrush. Since it was early spring and the area was still quite damp from the recently melted snow, he guessed that the fire would have to spread primarily through the canopy with the understory being so moist.

If he could find a low area void of trees for the right distance, he could survive almost any wildfire. His other option was to retreat to the river but not seeing any signs of wildlife fleeing the direction he was heading and not smelling the smoke any longer he carried on, just much more alert to his surroundings. As he came around another clump of dense cedars he stumbled upon a recently constructed car path through the forest.

He didn't think this was on his map. He kicked at the gravel on the path and looked both right and left in the direction of the cut through the woods. By the state of the road and nearby plant life, he guessed that the path had been made relatively recently. There were obvious signs of travel over the area as he noted some tire tracks on one side, a few metres away. In addition, the bushes and trees near the road had been recovering for at least a season or two based on the new growth he could see.

He twisted at his hips and brought his pack off his back, gently placing it on the road as he knelt down. He undid the front clasp and took out the topographic map of the area. He was not far from the last **X** he had marked on the map, indicating approximately where he had slept last night. It was a habit his father had taught him—track your path on your map and mark where you sleep each night, as well as other important sites. The information would come in handy if you had to retrace your steps.

He'd traveled perhaps half a dozen kilometers since he'd woken. The sun was well above the horizon by now and with the trees absent in this area, Dave could feel the sun quickly begin to warm him. He took off his outer jacket and tied it around his waist.

He laid the map out on the ground in front of him and traced a line in a general northeast direction from the clump of cedars he had slept behind. The map indicated nothing this close, no roads at all. He looked at the legend on the map. It was printed four years ago so the road was no more than four years old but likely two, Dave concluded. Might as well follow it, he thought, since it was going in the general direction he needed to travel.

Shouldering his pack and adjusting its weight, he began following the path through the forest. Periodically, Dave would see signs of small garden plots along the road. They all had the look of a child's touch. A sign leaned against a tree in one that said Kat's Garden, another hosted a gathering of Barbie dolls around a dining room table, and another a small home-made cross with the word Ginger written on it and a dog's collar laid on the freshly dug soil.

God, how do you explain what's going on to children at a time like this, Dave thought. It was hard enough for him to comprehend; he couldn't imagine having to deal with a child right now. How had his mum put it when she talked to anyone about her children, "Just waiting for this phase to pass; this living at home phase." Everyone knew she was only joking and loved her children passionately.

Dave stopped. He couldn't start thinking about his parents right now because he knew that only lead to dark places. He quickly brought his thoughts back to the here and now.

He noticed that the path was taking a slight curve just up ahead and wondered if he should continue following it when he caught the smell of smoke again, piquing his curiosity. Not twenty strides further on, the path suddenly opened up and he was looking at a small cabin with smoke coming from the chimney. What the heck, Dave thought.

Suddenly a child came running out the front door yelling at the top of her lungs. A screaming adult was running wildly after the child. He stared flabbergasted, as this was not what he was expecting when he awoke this morning.

He instinctively ran forward to try and protect the child, but then was struck by a thought. Shit, another black swan!

Boiling a frog is a metaphor for the problem we all have perceiving changes that are gradual but cumulatively significant, that may creep up and have devastating consequences: a little increase here, a little there, then later some more. Nothing changes very much and things seem normal. Then one day the accumulation of changes cause the appearance of normality to disappear. Suddenly things have changed a great deal. The world is different, and it has been altered in a manner that may not be pleasant.

Joseph Tainter & Tadeusz W. Patzek, 2012
Drilling Down: The Gulf Oil Debacle and Our Energy Dilemma

April 3, 7:30 a.m.

Shane felt the warmth of his wife's body as they lay together. Her long red hair was draped across his face, tickling his nose and waking him. He opened his eyes enough to see that the sun was already beginning to lighten the room.

He brushed Caera's hair aside then took a deep breath and slowly began to untangle himself from her embrace. As much as he would have preferred to remain right where he was, he knew he needed to get outside and begin expanding their vegetable garden.

Caera would want to get up as well but he let her sleep. The stress of the last few months had been enormous and he knew his wife well enough to allow her some extra sleep, for both their sakes.

As he put on some old clothes, something suitable for some heavy labour on this early spring morning, he thought about the situation he and his wife found themselves in. While difficult, Shane was thankful they had been transitioning to a grid-free lifestyle for the last several years. It was one of the main reasons that they had remained in their home as rolling blackouts began to sweep across the province on a regular basis. While it was worse south of the border, where oil dependency was larger and the economic situation much worse, Canada was seeing its own share of electrical load shedding, particularly in the eastern provinces. A limited supply of electricity was being shared among a growing number of customers.

As brownouts and blackouts became more common, most people in Shane's area had abandoned their homes to get together with family members in various larger towns and cities, especially provincial and territorial capitals where government support and resources were being concentrated. In fact, many suburban and rural families in general were migrating to larger centres where the government was trying to maintain constant energy supplies from basic electricity to fuel for cars, not to mention food.

Shane had not been able to pick up any news on any radio frequency for at least three months. He was sure that if there were no broadcasts, something significant had happened. But he had no idea what since no one was around to get information from, just one neighbour remained that he knew of. This was one of the hardest issues for Shane, not knowing what was going on in the rest of the province, or the world for that matter.

Prior to the seemingly permanent blackout they were now experiencing, the media had been reporting on the world's growing energy crisis. Blackouts had been sweeping through growing areas of the world for some time now as fuel to help keep generators running became too costly for most countries to afford. Pakistan and Venezuela had been experiencing rolling blackouts for more than a decade, as had most of India and China for the past several years.

News agencies had begun to investigate and report on rumours that the Saudis were contemplating a significant reduction in oil exports because of their own growing domestic energy demands.

Even just the rumour of this possibility was another stress the perpetually fragile world economy could not withstand. World markets crashed, again. Soon afterwards, blackouts that had been plaguing a limited number of countries for some time began to spread throughout the rest of the world.

The last report from the Canadian government that Shane had heard was from the prime minister, who had assured the Canadian people that their energy security was safe and that Canada would not succumb to the same fate as so many around the world. But it had.

Many in Canada viewed the situation in the Middle East as primarily an American concern, forgetting that eastern Canada was very dependent on oil from Middle Eastern refineries. About five months ago, brownouts began to sweep across the nation, beginning in the east. A month or so after that, rolling blackouts began to occur as the country struggled to keep pace with growing energy demand. After years of infrastructure neglect and questionable decisions by policy-makers and politicians, the grid was becoming less reliable.

This was about the same time that massive protests by the Occupier movement were planned in major centres. One weekend in early December about four months ago, the largest protests began. By the second day of the protest, the Toronto Occupier Riot—as the police, politicians, and media quickly called it, stressing *Occupier*—occurred.

It wasn't long after the Toronto riot began that all news reports stopped and were replaced by a simple repeated broadcast: 'This is a message from your provincial and federal governments. A state of emergency has been declared for all of Canada. We will advise you of further developments in the coming hours.' Shortly after that all grid power was lost in the area.

Shane paused and took a sip of his coffee as he looked out over his neighbourhood. The area was an eclectic mix of homes nestled around a small kettle lake, remnants of the mighty glaciers that once swept across most of Canada. The first homes built in the area had been simple cottages of a growing middle class during the early-1900s.

During those first thirty years of the twentieth century, Toronto's population had nearly quadrupled. It had quickly grown to a million people and some of them began to want to get away from the big city. Apart from farmers and loggers, few people ventured just north of the city. Within thirty minutes, one could escape the bustling city and travel back to a simpler time.

Some hundred years later, Toronto and area housed a population of more than ten million, depending on where boundaries were drawn. Those original 1920s cottages could now be found sitting between a late-twentieth century, thousand square foot bungalow and a twenty-first century, thirty-five hundred square foot McMansion. Progress is what some called it. Shane had other names for it.

Their home was a small one for the area—at just under eight hundred square feet—but it was a bungalow with a walkout basement. They couldn't have asked for anything better given the price at the time. The house actually provided them with far more living space than the two of them needed since they had dispensed with most of their material possessions when they moved to the area.

The hardest for Shane had been parting with his beer bottle collection. He had inherited it, of all things, from an uncle he used to have great fun with. Uncle M had been a full-time student of life; at least that is how he described himself. After receiving a PhD in cultural anthropology he had taken off to Southeast Asia. He had rarely come home since but when he did he always brought a few more empty bottles from wherever he had traveled.

He had had his father display them in their old, broken down garage near the back of their property. Shane had fallen in love with them after seeing them in that setting, covered in cobwebs and dust. It was the way the light shone through the broken window and cast a magical reflection of the different colours and shapes on the old car rusting under the roof of the garage.

It wasn't so much that he gave the collection up. After all, the bottles were back where he first saw them. It's just that he no longer had them displayed in his house where he could add to them more easily. He and Caera had agreed that only items that added productive value to the home or could serve in an emergency of some kind would accompany them. Shane had tried to justify their inclusion as backup drinking vessels, medicinal vials, rain collectors, bug prisons, urine receptors—his wife actually laughed at that one—and in his last-ditch attempt, as weapons, as he picked up a one and a half litre bottle from some former Soviet republic back in the 1960s and waved it back and forth in front of him.

"No you're right, honey," he finally admitted, frowning somewhat.

"And?" his wife added as she reached for his butt and pulled him closer.

"You're right dear. You're always right!"

"That's right and don't forget it," she whispered into his ear as she grabbed both cheeks in her hands and whispered something in his ear. He ended up being late for work that morning. He shook his head; back to reality buddy, he thought.

He and Caera had also made some significant renovations and additions to the property as they prepared to try and live off the grid. Thank goodness for one of his neighbours who had helped direct him towards all the resources to do the job properly. The changes they had made were serving them well now that their area had lost power.

The side hill had been terraced into a variety of garden plots capable of growing several types of vegetables. After having their asphalt-shingled roof replaced with a metal roof that was guaranteed for life, Shane had purchased a large quantity of rain barrels and created a drip-irrigation system using the rainwater collected by his roof.

With constant experimenting as to where to place the fifty plus rain barrels he had hooked up, he was able to have them all full at once. It gave them more than ten thousand litres of reserve water should they need it.

His wife thought he was crazy. Well he was crazy, right up until last year's mid-summer drought. That six-week drought, with the temperature hovering close to or above forty degrees Celsius every day, coupled with severe water restrictions due to already extra low lake and reservoir levels, had ravaged almost all of southern Ontario. Shane's watering system, however, had enabled him to keep all of his plants properly watered.

The torrential rainstorms that occurred for two weeks after the six weeks of drought made the impact of the drought significantly worse. Those rains ended up washing away so much fertile soil from Ontario farms that a provincial committee was immediately formed to look at best practices for trying to replenish all that lost soil. It was a 'once-in-a-lifetime' event that had had a devastating impact on Ontario's agricultural economy. The province had lost close to ninety percent of its agricultural potential during those two weeks of rain.

In addition to their watering system, Caera and Shane had built a cold cellar in their basement by sectioning off one corner and putting up insulated walls to form the room. They insulated the ceiling and removed the insulation from the cement walls of the foundation to allow the room to cool; an insulated door finished it off.

It was not a real root cellar and could only store a small variety of their garden harvest because it was still too warm. As their garden grew larger, Shane had constructed a real root cellar below the deck that came off their kitchen.

Wanting to act on his belief that he should employ the least energy-intensive means necessary when working around the house, he dug the entire area out by hand using a shovel and wheelbarrow. It had taken him about eighteen months, on and off, to dig out the soil as most of it had been hard-packed clay. He figured that he moved about fifteen-hundred square metres of soil during that time. As a result, however, he had lost a couple of centimeters off his waist, added a couple to his shoulders and upper back, and felt great!

Shane had followed all the books he could find at their local library on proper drainage, how to construct concrete block walls, pouring a concrete roof, and root cellaring. He learned that the ideal temperature for most root vegetables to over-winter was between zero and four degrees Celsius, and the best way to achieve and maintain that temperature was to dig well below the frost line. This meant going down at least three metres.

After all was said and done, he had a two hundred square foot root cellar that could serve as a storm cellar if need be. Since storms had been occurring more frequently and with greater force, as once-in-a-lifetime storms now seemed to hit several times every year, he was glad he had built it. Shane also stored all their emergency gear in the root cellar, leaving plenty of room to put up shelves for their harvested food.

They built redundancies into most of their vital systems, such as heating and cooling. They had added additional insulation to every wall in the house and the attic. They had installed both a wood and a propane-based fireplace; making sure both could also be used as stoves. Although each room had a ceiling fan, Caera and Shane preferred to use the basement on hot days and take advantage of the natural cooling that occurred with half the basement underground. On really hot days they would visit their root cellar for a while where it was a constant eight degrees.

Their electricity was generated by a small solar array on the roof, and a small wind generator near the back of the property. They had some gas-powered generators available, just in case—but limited fuel. They had not achieved zero electrical use but they were getting close. They knew they had to someday as there was always the possibility that all their systems could fail and not be reparable.

They had found that it was the little things that made the difference. Shane, for example, had purchased a straight razor blade and began using foaming soap bars instead of throwaway blades and cans of shaving cream, and he hadn't lost too much blood during the transition. Caera learned to make various meals using the food they grew and Shane began making bread from scratch, relying on the large store of flour they had accumulated. They used the solar oven they purchased a couple of years ago whenever it was sunny, and used an open fire to cook meat when they had it.

One of the first things they did after moving into their new house several years ago was to plant a variety of fruit trees in the part of the yard that received the best sunshine. They had at least six different species of apple trees, and several species of pear, cherry, and apricot trees. Since that first year they had also planted a variety of fruiting bushes including hardy kiwi, blackberries, blueberries, and raspberries.

Caera had been adding to the variety of crops they grew every year, adding two or three new vegetables to their harvest annually. They still had dozens of different seed packages to try and Caera had made sure they were all heirloom seeds, the kind of seeds that were open-pollinated and would produce the same kind of plant year-in and year-out. She shunned the hybrid crosses that attempted to bring out the best of both parents but what plant you got for the second generation was anybody's guess, if you even got any viable seeds. Grocery stores primarily sold the hybrid type of vegetables because they tended to be more visually-appealing than their heirloom cousins. What most people didn't realise, however, was that the heirloom vegetables were far more tasty and nutritious.

Shane reflected for a moment on the power grid situation. He had no idea what had happened to the electrical system in the area. Although energy issues had continued to get attention in the media and from the politicians, nobody seemed to be in any particular hurry. Canada had always been a country of vast resources and despite strong opposition the Canadian authorities had opened up broad areas of its northern land for mineral and energy exploitation as it attracted a lot of investment, particularly from China and India.

For quite some time Canada seemed to be insulated from the issues that were creating great stress in most other countries around the world, particularly in Europe, Japan, and Canada's southern neighbour, the United States. Canadian politicians and corporate leaders had cheered on the growth in free trade deals that continued to fuel the export of Canadian natural resources. The latest prime minister led Canada in a nationalistic cheer loosely based on Sir

Wilfred Laurier's famous words at the start of the twentieth century. "The twenty-first century is Canada's," he had stated and he was right, for a while. For a time, Canada led the world in exports through a huge increase in free trade deals; most of them centred on its natural resources, particularly fossil fuels and water. Money was flowing into almost every province.

Even Ontario, where things were looking pretty desperate for a while, had become a leader in shale gas production through novel and untested applications of an extraction method known as hydraulic fracturing or fracking. It was leading the way in extracting gas until an entire block in the city of London had exploded because of a leak of methane gas that had penetrated the city's water system from a nearby fracking site.

Despite assurances that this was an isolated case due to an unforeseen set of circumstances, it had set off a wild protest in London and surrounding areas that had stalled Ontario's fracking industry for some time. At least until it was nationalized a year or so ago; drilling sites and production rates were, among other things, now kept secret for purposes of 'national security'. National security, thought Shane, bullshit.

He had finally finished his coffee and wanted to get started. He put his cup down on his deck and walked out into the yard. Most recently he and his wife had been working on finishing up a new greenhouse they had purchased. It had been shipped in from a company in PEI last fall and the two large boxes that held it had sat in their garage all winter. It had only taken them about a day and a half to construct but, Shane remembered none-too-fondly, it had taken him several weeks in relatively cold late winter weather to construct the terrace for the new structure to stand on.

With the warming weather, they already had a number of seedlings started: corn, squash, peas, carrots, beans, radishes, cucumbers, and tomatoes. Corn and squash were new to the garden this year. As well, they had already started sweet potato slips and had regular seed potatoes to put in the ground once the soil was warm enough and all chances of frost had passed.

He gathered a pile of newspapers they had been saving from their weekend delivery of the *Toronto Star* and began to spread them over the grass. This would serve as natural control of the grass growth; it would kill the grass underneath and then decompose over time. Once he was finished the area they were expanding into, he would begin piling on some of their dwindling organic matter reserves. They had green compost from all their garden clippings and kitchen compost. Shane would also mix in some triple mix that he had left over from a local area landscape company delivery last fall.

It was frustrating, he thought, reflecting back on the energy issue again. Everybody knew the globe was facing an energy crunch. Ever since the first oil shock in the early 1970s, the globe was aware that the world's economic engine, the United States, needed the oil. They had become net importers at that time and began planning for their energy security during that decade. Most of this planning had been done in secret, but every once in a while a Freedom of Information request would get through or a leak would surface. *Wikileaks* had been great for uncovering corporate and government conspiracies, turning many conspiracy theories into conspiracy facts.

The evidence was overwhelming that the U.S. had made plans during the 1970s to control the world's oil reserves in various locations around the globe, but most importantly in the Middle East where most of the reserves were located. The plans included establishing stable governments, be they dictatorships or not, and a list of countries to control was made: Iran; Syria; Sudan; Somalia; Libya; and, Lebanon.

So long as the States got their oil, they cared little what the leaders of other countries did domestically. When a leader strayed too far from the American plan they would be ousted by whatever means necessary. One just needed to look at how Ghaddafi was vilified by ꞌ West and its media; he was accused of having weapons of mass ꞌuction and then conveniently murdered after being found.

Was his crime having weapons of mass destruction as the British and Americans declared? No, since there were no weapons of mass destruction ever discovered. The real issue seemed to be that Ghaddafi had been pushing for a gold-backed, Pan-Arab and -African currency to replace the American dollar and Euro for trade, especially of oil. The invasion of Libya had little to do with anything else, except maybe the one hundred and forty plus tonnes of gold in the Libyan Central Bank.

The Western oligarchs, in their attempt to keep the potency of their currencies, had just eliminated another threat; and one that just happened to be in the Middle East where twenty-five percent of the world's oil reserves was located.

Shane thought it was interesting how slowly things had appeared to be happening and then, as if someone had removed the plug that kept the tub from emptying, everything changed at once. One moment Canadian leaders were extolling that growth was improving and expanding and that we had turned the corner, then suddenly there seemed to be total chaos.

Massive public sector jobs were eliminated, creating a huge gap in public services that many citizens depended upon. The hospital where Caera worked as a critical care nurse was closed with no notice and all employees let go. Most doctors were quickly absorbed by the hospitals that remained open in the province, but thousands of nurses were dismissed. It appeared that as more and more people migrated to the larger urban centres, non-urban services were being slashed completely.

As a self-employed small engine repair specialist, Shane's business picked up as things began to deteriorate. Neighbours were fixing their appliances and motorised gadgets rather than replacing them at the first sign of problems, as had been too many people's default behaviour.

When gasoline prices began creeping towards ten dollars a litre, Shane saw a precipitous fall off in certain repairs such as lawn tractors and mowers, and most other gas-powered items. He had still received a lot of calls regarding other repairs, but that soon dropped off as well as fewer people remained in the area.

Caera had been providing some unofficial but necessary health-care for residents. She had collected the neighbours' extra first aid kits, and then organized and stocked their garage with everything brought. She had Shane help her set up the garage as a makeshift healthcare centre and dispensed first aid as required.

She had quickly studied all the resources she could find on medicinal plants and herbs, as she could not prescribe any medica-tions; not that many were available. Pharmacies had run out of most prescriptions due to supply chain interruptions. These interruptions were impacting grocery stores and a growing number of businesses as well, many of which were forced to close.

It was not surprising at all to Caera that next to a few cuts and bruises by the younger generation, stress seemed to be the biggest diagnosis. Most of the folks that visited really just needed some tender loving care; especially the adults, who seemed to be showing classic signs of post-traumatic stress syndrome. The children loved the fact that there was no school.

People offered to pay her but she declined any remuneration, even the food people began to trade as a means of local currency. She simply told anyone who sought help, "One day you might be able to help my husband and I, that's the only payment I need right now."

Then, in what appeared to come out of nowhere and with great speed, everyone was moving out of the area. As power outages became more frequent and longer lasting, the suburbs were quickly drained of most of its population. People, especially older retirees, were migrat-ing to their relatives in the closest capital. Early on, it was estimated that close to eighty percent of suburban and an increasing number of rural Ontario residents had moved into Toronto and Ottawa, where government services were beginning to be concentrated.

Neither Shane nor Caera had any siblings, and both had lost their parents some years ago. They had nowhere else to go and no one else to live with anywhere close by. There were a few distant aunts, uncles and cousins, but they were spread across the continent. With no transportation fuel to speak of, they were destined to survive where they were.

We'll be okay, Shane thought to himself, as we've learned so much these past few years. His reverie was cut short by a voice calling him, "Shane, you're out early to work on the yard."

Morpheus: The Matrix is everywhere. It's all around us, even in this very room. You can see it when you look out your window or when you turn on your television. You can feel it when you go to work, when you pay your taxes. The Matrix is the world that has been pulled over your eyes, to blind you from the truth.

Neo: What truth?

Morpheus: That you are a slave, Neo. Like everyone else, you were born into bondage, born into a prison that you cannot smell or taste or touch. A prison, for your mind. Unfortunately, no one can be 'told' what the Matrix is, you have to see it for yourself. (Morpheus opens a container that holds two pills: a blue one, and a red one. He puts one in each hand, and holds them out to Neo.) This is your last chance. After this, there is no turning back. You take the blue pill, the story ends. You wake up and believe whatever you want to believe. You take the red pill, you stay in Wonderland and I show you just how deep the rabbit hole goes.

Neo pauses for an instant, then reaches for the red pill. He swallows it down with a glass of water, and looks at Morpheus.

Morpheus: Remember, all I'm offering you is the truth: nothing more.

The Matrix, 1999
Warner Bros. Pictures. Written by Andy and Lana Wachowski

April 2, 7:00 p.m.

The setting sun sparkled off the small lake as Sam stood on his front porch and watched a few geese glide toward the eastern shoreline. As much as he'd love some fresh meat, Sam knew it was best to wait until after mating season before hunting any adult geese. Besides, he was on his way north tomorrow; he didn't have time to pluck the birds and cure the meat.

He looked west and wondered what his brother might be doing. They'd talked about this possibility many times. Sam had been warning Dave for years now that the world was heading for a massive social transformation. The signs were there for all to see: spiraling government debts, huge inflation in food and fuel prices, sovereign debt defaults, austerity programmes and their associated massive social protests, rolling brownouts and blackouts, rise of ultra-conservative governments and dictators, significant unemployment, and growing civil unrest worldwide. It had not been a good few years, to say the least.

Canada had been lucky up until now. Its history and geography had helped it to be one of the last countries to be impacted. But something has certainly impacted it, Sam thought.

Canada's bitumen reserves did little to cushion it from global energy issues. Fossil fuels had become an issue because too many countries had used up the last of their cheaply accessible oil and gas. The entire globe was now experiencing a fossil fuel resource crisis.

With growing gasoline and transportation fuel shortages, travel had ceased to exist in any recognizable form some months ago. Emergency services had been so overwhelmed they restricted themselves to being concentrated in each province's and territory's capital exclusively, and of course the national capital, Ottawa.

Sam had not seen or heard a commercial plane for at least a year. Commercial train service had been completely halted several months ago. Even military use of planes had ceased, followed shortly by the disappearance of military rail traffic. And, the last car Sam saw was that of his sister, who had arrived shortly after rail service had halted.

Unfortunately the last encounter with his sister, less than forty-eight hours ago, wasn't a great memory. They'd argued about a couple of issues, not least of which was his conviction to the idea that society was in rapid decline.

She had decided to go into Toronto. For Sam, getting further away from, rather than closer to, a large population centre such as the Greater Toronto Area was high on his list of things to do in order to survive. Sam was fairly certain that the transition would not go well...

"Dad, tell him!" Susie urged her father.

"You both have made some good points. However, Susie, I think Sam might be right this time," Joel Gregory stated, trying to apologise with his body language.

"It's pure logic," Sam chided his sister.

"There is absolutely nothing logical about forced birth control. It should be a choice," Susie stated categorically as she crossed her arms and refused to look at her brother.

"I didn't say anything about the morality of the issue, it's just that exponential growth of any species results in a catastrophic collapse of the-"

"Dad, Dad, I'm all done can I please be excused from the table? There's a golf tournament on!" seven-year-old Dave interrupted as he began to pick up his plates and head towards the sink.

"Yes, David. But please keep the volume down," Dave's dad replied.

"But humans aren't any species," Susie stressed. "They're capable of working together and building great things. We're smarter than any other species!"

"Depends on how you define smart," Sam replied.

Susie wasn't to be out-thought by her snarky, older brother. "We won't end up like other species because we can work together to overcome any problems. Local communities do this in the face of emergencies all the time."

"Yes, in certain circumstances humans are capable of wonderful things," her father added in support. "We have achieved space travel and amazing technology."

After a moment's pause, he continued. "We must remember, however, that humans are capable of vicious cruelty as well. Think about all the wars that have been fought, the bombs that have been dropped, and the landmines that have been planted. No, Susie, your brother is talking about mathematics, something that has no ethics, although it can be used unethically. The lesson he is trying to teach you is about exponential growth. It is perhaps the one lesson that most people fail to learn, especially our decision-makers."

"Think about this example, Susie," Sam began. "Let's imagine that you have a lab flask and inside you place a single bacterium that doubles in number every minute. And, let's assume it takes sixty minutes, or an hour, for the flask to fill with bacteria. We also need to imagine that the only resource this type of bacteria requires is space, with me so far?" Sam asked to ensure his sister was listening.

"Yes," Susie answered with as much attitude as she could muster.

"Okay, so if we place the single bacterium in the flask at 11:00 a.m., what time will it be when half, or fifty percent of the resource is gone, or fifty percent remaining?"

"That's easy, it's 11:59 a.m.," yelled Dave from the other room.

"Watch your stupid sports, you toad!" Susie yelled at him.

"Susan, not appropriate," her father gently scolded.

"Sorry, Dad. Sorry, David, that was uncalled for," Susie apologized to her brother.

"Ohhhhhhhhhhh, just missed an eagle," David shrieked, paying little attention to his sister.

"Susie, don't mind Dave," Sam interjected. "Okay, we've got half of the space remaining but only one minute left, agreed?"

"Yes."

"Good. In one minute the bacteria will be forced to either stop reproducing, as they have run out of space, or do what?"

"They could slow down their reproduction, maybe have some bacteria not reproduce; or look for more space," Susie quickly replied.

"Yes, all of those are possible. Let's look at the last option: look for more space. If they are able to double their space, say add another whole flask, how much more time does that give them?"

"Hm," Susie paused. "Oh, only one more minute."

"That's right. One whole minute was gained by doubling their resource. That's it, one minute or one more doubling," Sam stressed.

He paused, giving his sister time to comprehend the full impact of the example.

"I see," Susie stated as she began to understand the mathematics and physical limitations involved. "Because humans live on a finite planet with finite resources, we cannot continue to grow as we have been."

"That's right," Sam said smiling. "Now, think about this example not just for our ridiculous exploitation of natural and non-renewable resources, but try to imagine how this applies to the economy with the expectation of continual growth."

"When did economics enter the discussion?" Joel Gregory asked.

"I just started reading some great books and websites, and the same argument applies, Dad," Sam replied.

"I wish you wouldn't encourage them, Joel," called a voice from the other room.

"But Mum, this is really important stuff!" Sam piped up, replying to his mother's comment.

Marzia Gregory stepped into the room, removing her sweater as she walked. "It's important to you, not everybody," she said, as she ran a hand through Sam's hair.

"Mum, economics is important to everyone. It's the root of all evil, well, money is!" Sam stated emphatically.

"Is this what you've been reading? That money is evil?" she responded sliding a sideways look at her husband and blowing him a kiss. He winked back while pouring himself some more water.

"Well, I know that the phrase is used in the Bible. And Mark Twain has comedically—is that a word—twisted it to say that 'lack of money is the root of all evil', but actually I was doing some research on Libertarianism and began reading some Ayn Rand who used it in her book Atlas Shrugged and-

…Thinking for this long about his mother, Sam was jolted back to the present. Marzia Gregory had been seriously injured in a car accident over three years ago. The night she had been injured, their mother had taken the family car to run some errands. She had a list of grocery items, library books to be returned and a list of more books to pick up for her and her husband, and her husband's birthday list of tools from the local Home Hardware. On a quiet road, about halfway to town, another vehicle had run a stop sign and struck the Gregory's Mini Cooper.

The police would be investigating the accident but the family needed to know that their mother had been taken by air ambulance to a nearby hospital. Despite the fact that Marzia Gregory had remained in a coma since the accident, Joel Gregory had not left his wife's bedside for more than a day or two since. After three years in this condition, she no longer resembled the mother the children had remembered and all three had stopped visiting except during the traditional holiday season at the end of each calendar year. For all intents and purposes, their mother had passed away three years ago.

Susie had been staying with Sam the past couple of weeks but she had grown restless and was adamant that she was going to get her father out of Toronto. Just before she left, Sam gave his sister a small backpack. He told her to keep it with her at all times and, if she could, get back to his place with their father. With tears in her eyes, Susie hugged her brother one last time and turned to climb into her car.

"Thanks to you I've got enough gas to get to Dad but I don't know about getting back. I haven't seen an open gas station in months so it'll be awhile before I can make it back, but once everything is back to normal I'll give you a call," she sputtered through sobs.

There was no argument left in Sam. Susie and Sam had discussed the evidence for and against social change many times. Like him, she'd seen the data on world oil production and population growth; yes, she'd seen the research on climate change; and, yes, she had experienced prices spiraling out of control, especially food and fuel. She just couldn't believe, however, that it was the end of everything she'd struggled to protect.

Susie had become actively involved in her town's transition move-ment and had been instrumental in getting the community to begin a movement towards a lifestyle free of fossil fuel dependency. She was the optimist in the family and firmly believed all would return to normal soon enough.

"You do that, sis. Remember to keep that knapsack with you at all times. I love you." He didn't think the odds were good that he would ever see Susie again. If she kept the pack with her it could help, since she knew what to do.

"You know he's not going to come without Mum," Sam finally uttered.

"I know, but I've got to try. I love you." With that she closed the door and put the car in gear.

As she headed down his driveway and between the majestic spruce trees lining it, Sam couldn't help but think about how things had quickly disintegrated since his first public voicing of concerns about seven years ago…

Sam took a look out over the crowd. It was the usual eclectic mix of people, but comprised of mostly young adults, as most campus audiences would be. He'd been trying to get onto a campus for a couple of months now and had finally called in a favour. He emailed an old friend, Melissa Stanovic-Vanderhaule.

Sam and Mel had dated briefly as second-year students but discovered that a romantic relationship was not in the cards with both of them wanting to pursue very different career paths. He was set on moving out west to study archaeology and she was pursuing her M.R.S. degree. She'd misunderstood when he said he would be pursuing his doctorate. Sam was sure it was because of the noise in the pub when they chatted; it had nothing to do with the amount of beer being consumed in the student bar that night. Mel thought he meant he was studying medicine and they hit it off right away.

Mel's interest waned when she awoke the next morning and discovered he was not pursuing a medical degree. They'd stayed together for a few months and really did begin to enjoy each other's company. However, Mel was clear about her intention to find a man headed into medicine or dentistry. Despite this long-time obsession, she was a very intelligent woman and gifted mathematician. For some reason mathematics, all types, came naturally to her. While she was pursuing men, several universities were pursuing her to take up graduate studies on their campus.

She'd met Milav shortly before deciding on a graduate school. Milav was off to the University of Dallas, in Texas, home to the Texas Longhorns, to study medicine and Dallas had been pursuing Melissa along with everyone else. She took the opportunity and followed Milav; they were married eight months later. What Mel had not planned on was that Milav would end up as a university professor back in Canada as opposed to a plastic surgeon in California.

Honestly, however, Mel had never been happier. She and Milav had both attained tenured positions at the University of Toronto, with Milav doing medical research and Mel focusing on her role as Dean of Education, and working with the provincial government to rewrite and update the Ministry of Education's mathematics curriculum.

Mel glanced over at Sam as she finished his brief introduction, "-my friend, and sometime activist, Sam Gregory."

Sam stepped up to the lectern to some light applause. "Thank you, Dean Stanovic-Vanderhaule. Good evening everyone. It's my pleasure to be here this evening speaking to educators. I approached your dean last month about the possibility of getting onto a campus to share a couple of important topics and of course, you being educators, I agreed to weave my argument into a discussion about curriculum.

"The latest rage, I'm told, is basing curriculum on the knowledge and skills necessary for success in this twenty-first century. Without even getting into a philosophical debate about what defines success, I want you to think about what kind of curriculum might be important for your students if our view of the future is misguided or misinformed. What if we could be facing a **very** different future than the one we have been conditioned to believe we will encounter?

"Now, before I make some suggestions on the type of knowledge and skills that will likely be extremely important, given some minor but alternate assumptions about what the twenty-first century will look like, I want to focus on two others topics first: energy and money.

I hope to convince you that one cannot be discussed without the other and the future of these two issues will significantly impact the type of future your students are likely to experience.

"Actually, much of what I will share with you over the next hour or so should not come as a surprise. It is when we look at everything from a different perspective or paradigm, however, that we begin to see some really interesting things. Things, that if we look at the bare facts, appear to run in the opposite direction to what our global leadership has been telling us. Imagine that, politicians lying."

After everyone had stopped laughing, he continued. "I do need to warn you, however, that the line of thinking I want you to embark on over the next sixty or seventy minutes is likely going to challenge some of your more fundamental beliefs. As such, you may experience some typical reactions when someone calls into question your belief system. While individual reactions differ, a number of you will experience strong emotions in reaction to certain statements." Sam paused to take a drink of water, his throat already feeling dry.

"Some of you may be familiar with cognitive dissonance," he continued. "It's a phenomenon where exposure to information that conflicts with your beliefs will create internal discomfort. This discomfort is mitigated by altering your beliefs so that they more closely align with the new information, or by discounting/misinterpreting/refuting the information shared. Don't be alarmed by this, it is normal. What I'd like you to keep in mind is that it can also affect your thinking so try to overcome this instinctual response and just listen to the proposition. Then do your own research in order to confirm or discard the idea, rather than discounting it immediately, as the vast majority of people do because it challenges some strong beliefs," Sam paused to take another long drink of water and glance at his notes.

"Now, before I get too deep into my thesis, I'd also like you to remember that parable about the three blind men trying to describe an elephant from their contact with three very different body parts—a leg, the trunk, and the tail. Humans for all our intelligence never get the whole picture when we look at world events and history. In fact, one could argue that we are constantly getting only a fuzzy picture of how things work all the time. We fill in the ominous blanks based on past experience, knowledge, biases, and even our wishes sometimes. I would like you to try to keep an open mind during my presentation and save questions or comments until the end. Jot down ideas as I speak if something sounds odd or interesting and listen for explanations or points that address your concern.

"Now, let's place those caveats in the background and I'll begin by sharing two fundamental assumptions. And I need to share these assumptions because they form the foundation of my argument.

"First, I assume that we live on a planet with finite resources. Let's be honest, without access to extraterrestrial resources the planet has a limit to the amount of certain non-renewable resources such as water, arable land, minerals, and fossil fuels. Unfortunately, a lot of people don't consider these constraints important when picturing the future, especially economists," Sam expounded.

"Second, I assume that human population and its reliance on the aforementioned resources, particularly fossil fuels, have grown exponentially over the past several hundred years. All available data appear to support this second assumption.

"Now, you need to accept these two assumptions in order to better understand the remainder of my narrative." He paused, looked out over the group, noticing he hadn't quite hooked everybody yet so he forged on.

"I believe there is a **perfect storm** brewing which could see a global, social transformation unlike any seen before on the planet. This change will likely hit full speed in the next decade or two, possibly sooner. The shift will be caused by changes in two of our civilisation's most fundamental systems: our monetary and energy systems.

"These two complex systems have coalesced and created an impact on a third system, our environment. These systems are three very large fronts being blown together by gale force winds and will be the perfect storm in the not-too-distant future."

Sam noted that more of the students were beginning to show signs of increased interest, leaning forward and nodding now and again to certain points. He continued, gaining more confidence as time passed.

"If this storm is indeed on the horizon, then you as educators need to consider how best to prepare our future citizens. Will the future resemble the so-called knowledge economy the current system assumes? What if our current monetary system fails because of all the debt we've accumulated? What if the energy we rely so heavily on begins contracting as predicted? What knowledge and skills will be most important in one of these alternate scenarios?" He paused to take another drink and check his time.

"I would imagine some of you are beginning to think that I'm about to outline the end of the world. Let me be perfectly clear about the answer to this, yes and no." Everyone chuckled again.

"No, seriously folks, I'm talking about the end of one sociopolitical paradigm and the emergence of a different one; one that will be both simpler and more localised.

"I'm now going to share some rather interesting historical data to give this tale some context. At the end of the next hour I think you'll see that an unsustainable situation has emerged on our planet. Cutting to the chase, the simple truth is that it is only a matter of time before some very uncomfortable events begin to unfold. In fact, one could say have already begun to unfold. It would appear that we're going to experience a seemingly, never-ending contraction in human population and living standards throughout the world."

Sam heard some reaction to this last statement and felt the need to clarify.

"Again, that may sound apocalyptic but it need not be. It may be challenging and difficult but that's where the education system and its curriculum come in. Helping to teach our children how to over-come the impending challenges will be vital.

"Despite agreeing with the observation of Mark Twain that 'There are lies, damned lies, and statistics,' I'm now going to share the one graph that is perhaps more revealing than any other. It is a simple timeline showing human population growth up to just past the year 2000." He paused while nodding to the technician to display the first graph he'd brought with him.

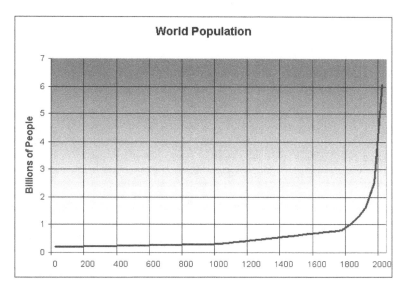

"As you can see, our species has **exploded** in size over the past several thousand years. Why has this happened? Well, some would argue that it was the domestication of edible plant species, followed shortly thereafter by our domestication of animals as workers and food. Others would state that our ingenuity has created a world that is safer and more aware of health issues than ever before. In truth, both of these variables probably contributed to helping us expand as well as several other factors in a complex system with various feed-back loops. I want to suggest another component, however, one that was probably the most significant contributor.

"On this next graph you will see another variable along with world population, that of oil production.

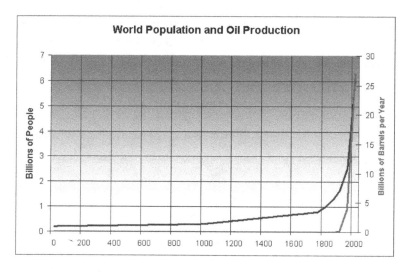

"You will notice at the end of the graph that the two variables overlap extensively. So, let's zero in on the twentieth century to see how the growth of human population relates to the growth of oil production.

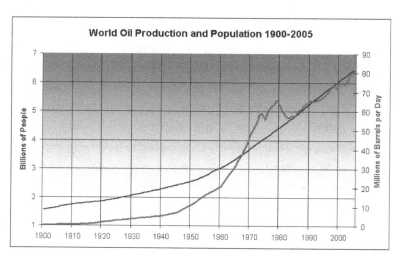

"Here you will notice that both world population and oil production rise together in a highly correlated fashion, especially since the mid-1980s. Obviously, correlation does not indicate causality; however, given the variety of agricultural, medical, and technological innovations that have been possible primarily because of fossil fuels, especially oil, we can be fairly certain that without such resources, we would live in a vastly different and less-populated world.

"Why are fossil fuels so important to human society? Essentially everything we use and depend upon in our globalised world relies upon the existence of fossil fuels, especially oil. But what is it exactly?

"This resource is basically a concentrated energy store: plant and animal matter that has been compressed and concentrated over time until we found it and began exploiting its energy potential. We've used it to replace human and animal labour. This, in turn, has allowed us to expand and grow in an almost unchecked manner, both in population size and environmental impact.

"Now, back to my first assumption: we live on a planet with finite resources. That would include fossil fuels. We know that these fuels will run out one day.

"But a bigger question that we need to consider is: What happens to human society and population after our oil stores begin to decline? If we haven't already passed oil's peak in production, as many argue—and remember 'Peak Oil' is not about running out of oil, as there will always be oil in the ground. Peak Oil is about running out of cheap-and-easily-accessible oil. It is about the human proclivity to use the easiest-to-retrieve resources prior to the harder-to-retrieve and, therefore, more expensive resources."

...That first presentation seemed a lifetime ago but it was less than a decade. Back then he thought he'd have a lot more time; no, he hoped he'd have a lot more time. Although the statistical models put any kind of social transition as further away in time and not happening so quickly, he knew that, as with any scientific prediction, nothing was certain; Heisenberg's uncertainty principle guaranteed it. As well, no prediction could account for a 'Black Swan' event—that totally unexpected event that changes all the variables beyond what anyone could foresee.

Sam drew his sweater's hood around his face a bit tighter to fight off the cold north-westerly wind. Hopefully the last blast of this winter, he thought. He was almost ready to head north. Susie had headed south but he had no idea where his brother might be.

The essence of the this-time-is-different syndrome is simple. It is rooted in the firmly held belief that financial crises are things that happen to other people in other countries at other times; crises do not happen to us, here and now. We are doing things better, we are smarter, we have learned from past mistakes. The old rules of valuation no longer apply. Unfortunately, a highly leveraged economy can unwittingly be sitting with its back at the edge of a financial cliff for many years before chance and circumstance provoke a crisis of confidence that pushes it off.

Carmen H. Reinhart & Kenneth S. Rogoff, 2008
This Time is Different: Eight Centuries of Financial Folly

December 12, 1:00 p.m.

Ranjeet sent the text and then powered off his BlackBerry, quickly shoving it into his bottom drawer just as his immediate supervisor walked into his office.

"Ranjeet, you know to keep this quiet, right?" George Stemmer, affectionately known as GS around the office, asked.

"Absolutely GS. Official announcement will be this evening after the west coast branches have closed. I won't talk to anyone," Ranjeet assured him.

"Tomorrow, then," George stated matter-of-factly, walking out the door and onto the next office.

Shit, thought Ranjeet, this can't be happening. He leaned back in his chair and summarized in his head the meeting his floor had just completed. At 7:00 p.m. Eastern Standard Time, all branches of all banks across the country were being temporarily closed. The government was calling a one-day holiday in order to perform yet another stress-test and make sure all banks were well capitalised. Given the rapid decline in other countries' banking systems for the past few months, the government was making a pre-emptive move to ensure and maintain confidence in the Canadian banking system.

Ranjeet understood the basic reason: Canada was preempting a bank run. But it didn't make sense since all the leaders and media had been playing up the improvements in the economy. Politicians were promising lots of infrastructure programmes to keep jobs growing in number, especially for the young Canadians who were finding it more and more difficult to find jobs but whose student loans were having to be paid back regardless of their financial situation.

Something must have happened to provoke the government and central bank to take this step, Ranjeet thought. Maybe there was a hint on one of the media websites. Ranjeet pulled over his keyboard and opened up a connection with the Internet.

He went to his bookmarks and scrolled down to CBC news and hit the link. Business news had the same storylines as the previous day: the Bank of Canada had promised to keep interest rates at zero percent for at least another year, avoiding the negative rate policies being followed by other central banks, but warned rates could move higher as well; the Minister of Finance was assuring Canada that trade deals with Asia would keep exports growing and jobs coming; and, a survey of leading economists predicted that Canadian GDP would begin to grow again once the current quarter was over—a few unforeseen events had caused a temporary contraction, but there were signs of improvement everywhere. Every other main media outlet he searched focused on the same narrow range of stories. There was no hint of anything out of the ordinary.

With no warning power was lost in the building and Ranjeet was staring at a dark computer screen. Not again, he thought. Sections of the province had been losing power on and off for the past few weeks. The government continually assured the public that they were investigating the power losses and would soon have everything under control and working normally again.

They had pointed fingers at a number of probable causes. Among some of the more popular in the news were: a significant decrease in water levels of lakes and rivers that provide hydroelectric power; increasing troubles with the American electrical system to which the Canadian grid was tied; and, a sudden, dramatic decrease in natural gas production across the continent, the fuel needed to keep gas-powered, electric-generators running. There were even rumours of Peak Uranium having been hit, thereby impacting nuclear power generation.

He could hear expletives from various offices around the floor as a few of his colleagues realised that they had probably lost the document they were working on. A few weeks ago, when they had experienced their second blackout in less than a week, Ranjeet swore to make sure he wasn't caught off guard again. He had only worked on an unplugged laptop for anything important since losing his whole hard drive because of the power surge that had precipitated that second blackout.

"Hey everybody, this is GS," George announced over the office intercom system, that would be powered for only a little while longer via the building's emergency generators. "Let's not end the week like this. It's two o'clock on a gloriously sunny Thursday afternoon. I understand that the temperature outside on this balmy December day is twenty degrees. I'm thinking maybe some patios might even be open. The last power outage lasted forty-eight hours. So, I'm going to suggest, no, I'm going to tell you all to pack your belongings and head home for the weekend. I will see everyone bright and early Monday morning. Have one for me," he ended. Everyone in the office knew that George had given up alcohol some years ago due to health issues but always ended his week's goodbye with that phrase.

Ranjeet grabbed his BlackBerry from his desk and headed for the stairs. Thank goodness they were going down the eleven floors and not up. It was apparent that a number of other floors were leaving the building early as well since the stairwell was packed with people heading down towards the lobby and parking levels.

"Hey, Ranj, wait up," came a voice from just above him.

He looked back for only a moment, not wanting to slow up traffic nor trip over his own feet, and saw the smiling face of Michael Choi, an old university buddy and now colleague at the bank. "Hey, Mike. How are things upstairs, in tech?" Ranjeet replied as he slowed, allowing a few colleagues to pass him on the stairs as Mike caught up.

"Pretty strange, I tell you. We just had a rather interesting floor meeting and now have been sent home for the weekend," Mike replied. "I'm assuming you too by your presence in the stairwell."

"Yeah, pretty odd don't you think?" Ranjeet asked.

"Nothing surprises me anymore, Ranj. Wait until you've been working here longer, you'll experience some pretty odd things, guaranteed," Mike paused for a moment then asked, "Hey, are you heading home right away?"

"I was planning on it. It's our date night and I thought we could get an early start. Nudge, nudge, wink, wink, say no more, say no more," Ranjeet mimed in his best British accent.

"Speaking of Monty Python, did you see that *Spamalot* is going to be playing again this summer?" Mike continued without a pause, "Margot's never seen it so I thought I'd take her. Do you think Chandra would want to go?"

"Not for a third time," Ranjeet replied, trying not to look too embarrassed.

"Okay, no double date to *Spamalot*," Mike announced and took a quick look around. "Have you got a few minutes to chat?" he asked, leaning in closer than normal to avoid being overheard.

"Is everything okay?" Ranjeet asked with some concern rising in his voice.

"Yeah, yeah, everything's great. Did you bring transit in today or walk?"

"I walked in, figured I could use the exercise," Ranjeet replied as he patted his stomach. "We've been able to leave the car parked for about six weeks now, ever since the price of gas passed the eight dollar a litre mark."

"I'll give you a ride home, it's on my way. Come on," Michael insisted as he steered Ranjeet through their building lobby, out the front door, and north on Bay Street.

"Wait, wait a minute," Ranjeet stopped cold. "I'm not on your way home. It'll add a good half-hour to your commute. I'm good to walk, really."

"Ranj, I need somebody to talk to and I'd like to do it away from anybody else's ears. It's not a problem for me; I need the extra drive time to think about what I'm going to do. Besides," he half grinned as he finished, "I've got one of the senior vice presidents covering my gas through some plan for the senior team. I just give him receipts and he has money transferred into my account."

"How'd you manage that coup?" Ranj asked, amazed once more by his friend.

"I helped him out with a technical glitch on his home network and security system a week or so ago. Anyways, I really need to share some things."

"This is sounding pretty serious. What's up?" Ranjeet enquired.

Before responding, Michael took another look around. The streets were busy with people and Ranjeet couldn't imagine what was bothering his friend so much. "I'll say more when we're in the car, Ranj. But, while we're walking let's talk about school."

"School?" Ranjeet replied.

"Yes, specifically economics. Remind me what constitutes a bank run," Mike replied.

"Come on, Mike, this is silly. I'm assuming you heard the same message during your floor meeting that I heard. What are-"

"Humour me please, Ranj," Mike interrupted. "You know I wouldn't insist unless I was serious. What constitutes a bank run?"

"Well, because banks use a system of fractional reserve banking, where they only keep a fraction of their assets as cash and on hand, if too many customers withdraw their money at the same time the bank can quickly become insolvent through a crisis of confidence, or positive feedback loop where people see others taking their money out and suddenly feel a need to do the same before the bank does run out of actual money.

"This escalates to a point where the bank has to close its doors, either to stop the run or because they are bankrupt. There's a great example in that classic Jimmy Stewart movie, *It's a Wonderful Life*. It's one of my favourite Christmas movies; after *Elf* of course!" Ranjeet concluded.

"'Is there sugar in syrup? Then YES!' Love that movie and maple syrup of course. Great, and how about a banking panic?" asked Mike.

"Okay, extend a single bank run to most or all of the banks and you have a panic. This is what is thought to have contributed significantly to the problems during the late-1920s and early-1930s, and just a couple years ago in Europe. I have a feeling I know where you're going with this; you think it's going to happen to us. But we've been through this I don't know how many times in the office, Mike. We've put enough regulations and firewalls in place to ensure it doesn't happen here. Banks have been recapitalized and numerous stress tests have all produced positive results."

"Yes and the people in charge never, ever lie," Mike retorted while rolling his eyes. He steered Ranjeet into the parking lot he had parked at and towards his car. Mike popped the locks with his remote and they both got in.

"Some buddies and I have been hacking around. Here hold this please," he asked, passing Ranjeet a bottle of water he had been carrying but had not begun drinking yet. "Anyways, it looks like a banking crisis started in the States a few days ago, something about their shadow banking system collapsing. I've only got some bits and pieces of news but given what appears to be happening to the south, I think our government is stepping in preemptively to prevent it from spreading here. We have a lot of liabilities with American banks and just look at the losses we suffered when the Euro collapsed.

"Anyways, if the government follows the playbook of the other countries that have recently tried to prevent the same type of runs and failed, then we're first looking at some pretty draconian capital controls being imposed before they allow the banks to be open again."

Mike picked up a CD case by Ranjeet's feet, opened it, and slid the CD into the car's CD player as he started his car, tossing the case between the two of them. Just before he reached the pay booth the music began. It was a song Ranjeet didn't recognise and it had some rather haunting lyrics, given the conversation so far. Ranjeet focused on the words as Mike had a short conversation with the booth operator.

When everything seems either funny or lousy, funny or lousy, that's where it usually ends.

From until we're no longer fun to that's no longer relevant.

From until we're no longer one to that's no longer permanent.

From the last survivors of those terms to the bona-fide embodiment of an endless emergency without end.

We're an endless emergency without end.

We're an endless emergency without end.

An emergency without end, that's exactly what Mike was implying. He picked up the CD case and looked at it: *The Tragically Hip, Day for Night*. He flipped the case over and read the songs; 'Emergency', that had to be the title.

He laid his head back on the seat and thought about Mike and his endless emergencies, and conspiracy theories. Without thinking about it, he unscrewed the cap on the water Mike had given him and took a few gulps. It had been fun back in university to argue and debate possible conspiracies, but Ranjeet had abandoned such skeptical thinking shortly after graduating and joining the banking industry at a branch close to his home. Questioning the philosophy and ethics of banking was not something someone within the banking world did as a matter of habit.

Mike, however, did not come to banking with the same background and training that most people did. He was a technological genius and while taking some undergraduate business courses, he had majored in computer studies and philosophy.

Ranjeet looked at his friend and thought, he's crazy but he's also a brilliant systems thinker. He wanted to challenge his friend a bit so he attempted to counter Mike's argument. "Okay, our exports should be stable enough to see us through most any crisis. Everybody needs our commodities; our oil and gas, and especially our water the last couple of years."

"In an ideal world sure, and within the narrative being sold to us by the authorities. However, there seems to be far more going on here than we're being led to believe. First, it seems pretty clear that oil production in Saudi Arabia, the world's leading producer and exporter, peaked a few years ago. The problem for them now is that in order to meet domestic demands they're looking at halting all exports, something that the global economy can't afford. What may be worse for Canada, however, could be the posturing going on between us and the States near the border in the western provinces. It doesn't look good."

"There's been none of this in the media, Mike. You're seeing ghosts and probably reading some hacker's fiction," Ranjeet stressed.

"Ranj, remember when we used to debate the causes of the Euro break-up, beginning with the 2008 sub-prime mortgage crisis in the States. During those years we witnessed bank runs, bank panics, social chaos, and political brinkmanship, amongst a host of other unintended consequences. Think back to those arguments. We both know that European leaders were lying constantly. Cooked financial statements, the LIBOR scandal, shadow banking, rehypothecation of assets that resulted in extreme leverage of the system beyond anything ever imagined, and off-balance-sheet transactions that have never been made public."

"Yes, but we both also know that Canada, has under the guidance of our central bank, regulated the system such that we have conquered our debt problems arising from the 2008 crisis and will not allow it to happen here."

"What if, however, there were unintended consequences of our changes that hadn't been realised until now? What if, for example, the deregulation of environmental assessment ended up resulting in the destruction of the country's most fundamental commodity: water?"

"What? This is as bad as your conspiracy theory around 9/11 or Kennedy's assassination, Mike. It's not going to happen here."

"I tell ya, the CIA killed Kennedy before he could expose some of their dirty laundry. Regardless, you have to stop drinking the kool-aid these guys are handing out, buddy," Mike countered. "Start being just a bit skeptical again. The leaders all have God Complexes; they believe they are not only omniscient but omnipotent."

"I think they have pills for that last one, you know," Ranj interjected, smiling at Mike.

"Omnipotent not impotent, seriously man look, these people think they can control a highly complex system like global economics and prevent any negative impact. They can't and they still haven't learned that. The stuff I've been reading would scare the shit out of most people," Mike continued getting more upset as he spoke. "The-powers-that-be have been suppressing dissent for ages and they still are. Ask yourself why the press NEVER disagrees with the government anymore? Why, after passing legislation meant to prevent external threats, most Canadian security laws are now focused inward on its own citizens? Why-"

"Where are you getting all this information?" Ranjeet asked.

"Online-"

"How are you getting past all the government firewalls that have been implemented the past few years?" Ranjeet interrupted.

"Yeah, the government certainly pulled the wool over everybody's eyes with those never-ending omnibus budgets the past few years, didn't they? Every one of those bills slipped more censorship laws in place and when that failed, what did they do?" Mike asked rhetorically. "They nationalized the service providers, but remember who you're talking to," he ended, looking like it was all a piece of cake.

After a moment's pause he continued. "Listen, this is far worse than the media and politicians have made it out to be. Things are about to go south real quick. Are you guys able to get out of the city?"

"Get out of the city? Why?"

"If things get as bad as we think, you could see the Occupier protests that they've just called for this weekend make the Quebec Spring look like a family picnic. Remember how that ended up. They thought everything was settled then **boom**! We see the first use of the *Emergency Management Act:* the immediate loss of most civil liberties across the province. Despite those measures being temporary, word is most of the laws are still in place within Quebec."

"It's different here, Mike, that won't happen; it can't happen." Raneetj was beginning to worry. He and Chandra had just purchased a new home in the suburbs to replace their small condo that was right in the core of the city. He told himself that Mike was just exaggerating. He saw conspiracy theories everywhere and could talk himself into a frenzy.

Ranjeet knew this, but he also knew that laws regarding the assembly of people and political dissent had been changing. The shift was rather slow at first but more recently changes were happening quite quickly as the government began implementing monthly omnibus bills.

The most bizarre legislation, Ranjeet thought, was their recent labeling of the David Suzuki Foundation as a terrorist organisation and arresting several members of their board of directors. The government brought forward evidence during the ensuing trial that members of the foundation's board had been working closely with Native groups that had been found guilty of sabotaging oil and gas pipelines. The defense argued that the evidence was fabricated but the court found the Foundation members and, by extension, their organisation, guilty all the same.

Crises in other countries did seem to be occurring much more frequently as well, but the media was always stressing the stability and success of Canada. Their growing export base, especially clean water, kept them as the darling of the world's trade centres, which had increasingly become more Asian.

The message from Canadian leaders was that Canada was different than everywhere else that was experiencing difficulty. Ranjeet felt comfortable believing this narrative; it lent stability to his life.

"Here are a few files I printed to share," Mike said, interrupting Ranjeet's thinking. "Burn them after you read them. They're toxic, worse than the radiated fish they keep pulling from the Pacific. Fukushima, wasn't that a nightmare. Reports are it's been getting worse, not better like we've been told. One American scientist has shared that if things continue on their present course, she is moving her entire family to the southern hemisphere; it's that bad."

Ranj brought his face up from the papers Mike had just handed him. "How can I know this isn't some prank, Mike? Some hacker's joke? How-"

"Just read the files, buddy. Listen, I'd sit under the TV for this one," Michael offered.

This was serious then, Ranj thought. Mike rarely was sure of anything. Offering to 'sit under the TV' was another way for their group of friends to affirm they were one hundred percent sure something was true. The saying arose a number of years ago when they used to play a popular online trivia game that was watched on old television sets, LCD displays, and the like in many pubs and bars across the continent. One evening while they were enjoying a few pints and playing trivia in their favourite location, a large, older-style television set suspended from the ceiling had fallen from its support and crushed the table over which it was perched. Luckily no one was sitting at that particular spot that night but since then they had offered to sit under the TV if they were certain of something.

"A few of the more interesting ones for Canada are on top," Mike continued. "First and foremost, for those who rely on trade with the States, like Canada, is that China finally appears ready to make a move to replace the U.S. dollar as the world's reserve currency with a gold-backed renminbi. Since they already have currency swap agreements in place with most of the world, it should be an easy transition. As you can imagine, the Americans are apoplectic! I can't imagine the world's biggest military machine sitting back and losing that privileged position without putting up a fight. But reserve currencies don't last forever. Ask Britain, Spain, and the Netherlands.

"Adding to that is the disaster that seems to have befallen the American shadow banking system. When it almost collapsed in 2007 we know what happened: the subprime mortgage crisis and the bankruptcies of Lehman's and AIG. Well, looks like it has imploded this time. Global credit is about to collapse and you know what that means.

"As for our exports, there is growing talk that our water is showing significant levels of toxic chemicals, especially those used by our oil and gas industry. Countries have been testing and then refusing our water for the past few weeks, meaning our resource bubble is about to pop and likely bring our whole economy down with it. The Council of Canadians warned us years ago to protect our water. We should have listened.

"The other big one that could have serious consequences for the world is the tension between a number of European countries; tension that has been building since their monetary union collapsed. I won't even get into what's happening with respect to the disaster continuing in the Middle East, except to say that Russia and China have put troops on the ground in Iran."

They had been sitting at the curb for sometime but Ranjeet had just noticed they were in front of his building. He realised that there was some validity in Mike's argument. With a loss of only about five percent of exports, the Canadian economy would move from a surplus to a deficit situation. A larger loss would be far, far worse. Canadians were still the 'hewers of wood and drawers of water' as characterized by economic historian Harold Innis in 1930. Export of natural resources was still everything for the country. Little had been done over the years to change this dependency.

"This global, fiat-currency Ponzi scheme is about to collapse and there's nothing that any central bank or government can do about it. It's time to get out of Dodge, buddy!"

"Mike, you said that when JP Morgan collapsed in the States not long ago. There were some trying times then, but we pulled through okay. Our banking system is even stronger and better prepared this time."

"Okay, you're the economist right? Take a look at the paper about banks' tangible common equities. You and I both know this is a measure of a bank's ability to absorb losses. The list in that pile shows the worst twenty-five global banks with respect to a TCE ratio; and thirty percent of those banks are Canadian, more than any other country, even more than the States."

"Are you doing this to scare me or what? You know Chandra and I just bought a house," Ranjeet pushed back.

"I know I've cried wolf before but I'm really worried this time. Have I ever offered to sit under the TV before? Look, I know this is going to sound even crazier than usual but I'm even starting to think that our leaders are behind today's power failure and the early closure of the banks. I'm guessing that an announcement will be made before the banks open Monday, stating that this temporary closure will be extended. They'll come up with some excuse, maybe something to do with the ongoing power disruptions and lock us out."

"Okay, on that conspiratorial note Mike, I've got to go," Ranjeet stated as he opened the car door.

"Ranj, read those print outs and think about what I've said. It's pretty serious this time."

"Mike, I'll read them but I'm not promising that I'll drink **your** kool-aid. I will try to keep an open mind and we can chat on Monday at work. Let's do lunch."

"I don't think we'll be at work on Monday, but if we are sure. Take care, and be safe pal!"

"You too, Mike. Thanks for the lift." With that, Ranj closed the car door and turned towards his building. Once inside he automatically headed for the elevator and pushed the up button. It wasn't until someone came out of the stairway door that Ranjeet remembered the power outage. He'd certainly get his exercise today, he thought, as he began his ascent to the twenty-third floor.

He took out his BlackBerry and powered it up. At least it was still functioning. He typed a short text to his wife as he climbed the stairs, letting her know that he was home early and had been given a three-day weekend due to the power loss. He knew she was home as she had not gone into her classes today because of a doctor's appointment.

A minute later he received a reply text: *Glad you're home, I have a surprise.* That's all he needed, another surprise today.

Somewhat winded and with aching calves, he finally reached his floor and unlocked his condo door. Chandra was waiting by the door and handed him a small gift bag as he entered, urging him to open it with her body language.

Before he opened the bag, he asked his wife, "Did you get to the bank and empty the safety deposit box?"

"Yeah, I still don't understand but I did it and everything's in the bedroom. Open the gift bag, please," she urged. She studied him closely as he reached into the bag and brought out a cigar box.

Why on earth a cigar box, he thought. He opened the box and it hit home like a tonne of bricks. Inside the cigar box was a single Cuban Cohiba cigar and a positive pregnancy test.

Bob Lee Swagger: Don't really like the President much. Didn't like the one before that much, either.
Colonel Issac Johnson: You like the idea of the President? Living in a free country? Do we allow America to be ruled by thugs?
Bob Lee Swagger: Sure, some years we do.

Shooter, 2007
Paramount Pictures. Screenplay: Jonathan Lemkin; Novel: Stephen Hunter

October 15, 7:00 p.m.

"Where the hell are we?" MacIntyre McKenzie, better known as Mac, asked his Lethbridge College classmate as he slowly shifted his gaze away from the scene rolling along on the highway outside his window. He had his window down a few centimeters so that the smoke from the joint he had lit would get drafted out and away from the car's interior. There was still a slight haze, however, as he squinted at the car's driver, Lazzaro Cutri.

"I'm sure there'll be another sign coming up soon but I know we're still on Highway 500. It can't be far," Laz replied.

"I hope not 'cause it's gettin' late. Where do you wanna start tomorrow?" Mac asked.

"Well, I'd love to see some of the petroglyphs. Writing-on-Stone Park or Áísínai'pi, as the Blackfoot natives call it—and I have no idea if I am pronouncing that even remotely right—hosts the largest concentration of rock art on the plains."

"Yea, that's cool," Mac responded. "I read that. You know I come from an area that has Native petroglyphs close by. But in Ontario we have much more original names for parks than Writing-on-Stone. We call it," he said in as straight a face as possible, pausing just strategically long enough and pronouncing each word precisely for full comedic effect, "Petroglyphs—Provincial—Park."

Laz chuckled as he took another sip of water. "I don't know if Writing-on-Stone is any better; however, you have to admit that both are pretty precise. Listen, you packed all the gear, right? I don't want to be all the way out here in the middle of nowhere and have to turn around and go back to the college."

Mac took another drag on the joint he was holding and as he exhaled answered. "Yes, everything is there: both cameras, video and still; extra batteries for both cameras; and, a couple of beers."

"Uh, out the window please, I'm driving," Laz reminded Mac, as he tried to fan some of the smoke back towards Mac's side of the car.

"Sorry, man. Listen, I wouldn't mind spending some time looking at the rock art as well but what caught my eye was the landscape. All those coulees and hoodoos."

"Remind me how that happened again," Laz prompted.

Taking on a more formal tone, Mac explained. "According to the material I read, the area used to be at the edge of a huge inland sea where a lot of sand was laid down over time. Over millions of years this sand was compressed into sandstone. During the last ice age, the retreating glacial melt-water eroded the sandstone to form these gullies and ravines known as coulees. However, when a harder substance protected an area of sandstone you got some neat erosion happening, and that's what formed the column-like structures: the hoodoos. It looks really cool in the photos I saw."

Falling back into his less formal speech, he continued. "So, how'd ya arrange the personal tour, anyways? I thought the park had been closed. You know, off-limits to the public since border issues flared up."

"My cousin worked at the park before they closed it and she owed me a favour. I gave her a call and explained the class assignment, playing up the whole interactive project angle. I asked her for a quick tour to get some exclusive video footage and she agreed. I also begged her to walk us through and share everything she knows about the park. I told her she didn't have to be on film; just the voice would be fine."

"She, huh?" Mac thought out loud.

"Forget it, Mac. She's my cousin and you need to focus on the assignment, not the girl. Besides, she has a **big** boyfriend," Laz warned. "There's a sign for the park, five more kilometres. Did you bring anything besides beer? We're going to be here for three days."

"Yes I did and as long as we have something over our heads, I've got everything else we'll need; more than enough for three people for three days. I used to camp all the time growing up. We'll be fine. Did you do **your** part?"

"Yes sir, it's in my knapsack so just hold tight. Are you okay if I, ah, ask you a personal question?" Laz enquired apprehensively.

"Go ahead and ask, I'll answer dependin' on how personal we're talkin', pal," Mac said as he gave his classmate a sidelong glance.

"What is somebody," Laz paused searching for words that would not offend. "Somebody of-"

"My age?" offered Mac, seeing Laz struggle.

"Well, sure, age. What is somebody of your age doing in this programme? Multimedia production is not usually something older students go into; at least not full-time, and not in a strange province."

"I'll answer that in time but I'd rather talk politics, if we're going to chat," Mac replied as he took a final hit from the joint he had now finished smoking.

"Why politics?" Laz asked glancing over at his classmate.

"I love talkin' about politics when I'm stoned. Hey, where's that beer?" he asked, twisting around to look into the back seat.

"Not until we're in the park and out of the car; my car, my rules," Laz stated.

"Okay, no beer, but you always need something to drink when discussin' politics. It helps get you in the mood for a good argument, or fight," he added while grinning, and pointing to the chipped tooth he sported.

"You're a crazy bastard, you know that," Laz said lightly, shaking his head as he said it.

"Look, life is about politics, Laz. Whether it's the politics between two lovers, or a mother and daughter, or an employee and his employer; it's all about politics. For the sake of the young and naïve, such as you, we'll stick to international current events. How's that?" Mac offered.

"Okay but I don't follow politics too much. To be honest, I know who the major leaders are, but I lost faith in the system long ago. Most people I know my age don't bother voting or following politics. It's just about fraud, corruption, nepotism. You know, politics."

"I can see how young people could come to that conclusion. In fact, I'm surprised more people haven't adopted that attitude given that they don't even try to hide their malfeasance anymore."

"Their mal-, mal- what?"

"Sorry, Laz. Malfeasance refers to a public servant acting illegally. I used to think that our democratic system was the **epitome** of political systems, at least until I was about nineteen and began to see more and more fascism creeping into the system," Mac argued, as he took on his more formal tone again.

"Fascism? Pretty strong condemnation, don't you think?" Laz asked, wondering where his classmate was going with the conversation.

"Okay, just take a bit of time and think about some of the changes that have taken place over the past couple of years. We've seen more and more interference in the economic system. Major governments the world over have been manipulating the global market for years and it has now become not only expected but necessary in the eyes of many investors; even here, in Canada. What bothers me more is the increased militarization of our country, especially in this part of Canada."

"It's to protect our oil and gas infrastructure. I know that much," Laz replied, feeling confident in his perspective.

"Protect it from what?" Mac challenged.

"Terrorists," Laz answered, replicating the answer the media and government had been repeating constantly.

"Terrorists? Tell me, Laz, how would you, you know, recognise a terrorist? Or, better yet, how would you define terrorism?" Mac asked, becoming more animated again.

"Well, terrorism would be any act that puts the public at risk," Laz replied.

"So, would you label the Council of Canadians or the David Suzuki Foundation a terrorist organization, as our government just did?"

"I heard that they were helping Native groups sabotage pipelines in the area. That certainly qualifies," Laz countered.

"Pipelines that, despite government propaganda to the contrary, cross a lot of Native land with no agreements or remuneration for the Natives. Not to mention-" Mac argued.

"There's the entrance. Ernie's going to meet us here," Laz interjected as he pulled his car off the road and parked in a shaded area of the small parking lot.

"Ernie? Is Bert coming too?" Mac asked in jest.

"Short for Ernesta," Laz replied as he turned off the car and opened his door. "Who is Bert?" he asked.

Mac smiled. "Forget it," he said as he opened his own door. "We're outta the car so pop the trunk if you would my man. I'm grabbin' a beer now, you want one?" Mac asked.

"Not yet," Laz responded. "If you brought any water, I'd appreciate some of that. What a beautiful day, thank goodness for yet another extended summer. You never know what turn the weather will take anymore," he added as he got out of his car and stretched.

"Back to terrorism," Mac started, as he handed Laz a canteen full of water and leaned against the car hood. "It's another emotionally-charged topic. Don't you think it's a 'coincidence' that many nation-states will not agree on a definition of terrorism? I think that's purposeful."

"What's made you so cynical?" Laz asked with a raised eyebrow.

"Experience my lad. I used to believe that government was a responsible institution, but just think about this whole concept of terrorism for a moment. I believe that governments have purposely left it open to interpretation; that way it becomes whatever they want. A great example was the way the Obama administration redefined who were terrorists or militants. During their ongoing invasion of the Middle East evidence emerged that they were assassinating innocent civilians, including children.

"Maybe you remember the video that *Wikileaks* published showing a family with children coming to the aid of some journalists that had been wrongly identified as potential targets and strafed by American fighters. Not only did the Americans ensure any target still moving was further strafed, but the van with the children inside was pulverized as well, killing the children and any other occupants.

"So, rather than review their overall mandate, they simply charged the alleged whistleblower with treason and changed the rules. In order to minimise the statistics around civilians killed—or 'collateral damage' as they sometimes call it—they decided to redefine what a 'terrorist' is. Now it is any person coming to the aid of a target, or, better yet, any person attending a terrorist's funeral.

"I mean really, it's just about making their killings and lies look justifiable. Noam Chomsky referred to it as 'manufacturing consent'. You know, getting the public behind government actions even when those actions could be viewed as terrorism or crimes against humanity themselves. If we look at the facts, the United States sponsors more international terrorism than any other country on the planet."

Mac paused and took a sip of beer. He was starting to get into his rant. "As well, military spending across the globe has increased every year since 9/11. It doesn't matter that the world is experiencing the worst global depression and highest unemployment in history. I don't know about you, but I don't feel any safer. In fact, I'm convinced we've given up so many freedoms that the government could do anything it wanted and find a law to make it legal; or quickly pass legislation to make it illegal—retroactively.

"The Canadian government has been closely imitating the Americans in these laws. The U.S. government has removed so many civil rights since 9/11, it's scary; all in the name of 'safety', of course."

"Well, what do you think is happening?" Laz asked, as he grabbed his knapsack from the backseat and then wandered around to join Mac.

"Well," Mac began and then paused taking a moment to gather his thoughts and finish off his beer. "I believe it's all about the oligarchs consolidating power. Let me list some of the laws that have been implemented south of the border over the past few years as evidence. Now don't get me wrong, this is completely non-partisan as it hasn't mattered whether it was Democrats or Republicans in the States; or Conservatives or Liberals here in Canada. Regardless of political stripes, sovereign states across the globe have been tightening their grip on personal freedoms for years-" Mac began, waving his hands here and there to accentuate his concerns.

"Here," interrupted Laz, as he threw him a bag.

Mac caught the bag, opened it up and stuck his nose in, inhaling deeply. "**You** are the man!" he stressed, as he leaned forward to give Laz a fist bump. Mac reached into his jacket pocket and pulled out some rolling papers. Placing the bag of newly acquired Cannabis on the hood beside him, he took out a single rolling paper.

"In reality, well, my reality," Mac snickered, as he reached into the bag he had just received and pulled out a clump of leaves, "I would argue that the United States has been tilting towards fascism for decades. For example, Ronald Reagan signed into law the *Military Cooperation with Law Enforcement Act* in the early-1980s. The name says it all: it 'encouraged' the military to cooperate with police forces by supplying them with hardware, training, and other necessary resources.

"Since that time, American police forces have received tens of thousands of M-16 assault rifles and M-14s, hundreds of grenade launchers and tanks, dozens of helicopters, planes, armoured personnel carriers, and anti-missile launchers. My favourite, though, would be the thousands of bayonets. What the hell do the police forces need these for? Bayonets? What do you think? Do you think domestic law enforcement agencies need these things?"

"I really haven't paid much attention to that stuff. I have no idea why police forces would need such weapons," Laz stated, creasing his brow in rising concern.

"The authorities would like everyone to believe it's to protect citizens from the terrorists hiding amongst them. The American military even began performing exercises in major cities not too long ago to acclimatize its citizens to the presence of the military. I think this whole situation has been planned for decades.

"If you look back in history, you see that plans to increase domestic security were mostly written up during the late-1970s and early-1980s. In fact, the now infamous *USA Patriot Act*, or to give it its proper name, the *Uniting and Strengthening America by Providing Appropriate Tools to Intercept and Obstruct Terrorism Act*, further eroded civil rights and freedoms.

"But the latest legislation, the *America First Act*, puts all the rest to shame. In short, it gives the president of the United States monarch-like powers: complete discretionary power regarding decisions without answering to **anyone**. Not Congress. Not the Supreme Court. No one! In addition, the president can ignore any law, past or present."

"Doesn't that make decision-making easier for a country's leader?" Laz offered, basing his comment on the little he had read in the mainstream media.

"Come on, really? These guys already think they're above the law, they don't need supreme executive power—ha, ha," Mac began chuckling.

"What?" Laz asked.

"I'm reminded of a scene from one of my favourite movies, *Monty Python and the Holy Grail*. My nephew and I used to recite this skit from the movie that cracked us both up. Let me see if I can pull the memory from the old hard drive," Mac said between giggles.

He took another drag on his joint before he began. "Okay, imagine two peasants working in the middle of a field collecting cow paddies-"

"Why would they be collecting cow paddies," Laz asked, feigning disgust.

"That's a great question," Mac said standing erect suddenly. "The answer is actually at the heart of this global crisis we've found ourselves in the past few years: **energy**. They were collecting cow paddies for one of two reasons. In medieval times peasants would collect cow paddies to dry out and then burn as fuel; or they would use them as a means of fertilizing their crops," he explained as he leaned back against the car again. "Anyways, they're in this field collecting cow paddies and the king of England, King Arthur, rides up to them and asks the man working in the field about the nearby castle-" Mac stopped himself abruptly. "Ask me to finish the skit for you another time, I think our tour guide is here," Mac said, as he pushed himself away from the car and pointed to the car turning into the park.

An older model, blue Fortwo slowed and turned into the entrance. The driver parked beside Laz's beat up Focus and popped out.

"Ernie!" Laz exclaimed, as he walked over to give his cousin a hug and kiss on each cheek.

Mac followed right behind Laz and introduced himself after Laz let Ernie out of his embrace. "Hi, I'm Mac. Ernie, correct?" Mac asked, as he offered his hand for an introductory shake.

"Yes, hi," Ernie replied. "I guess we're doing some homework, right?" she offered in return and then spoke to her cousin. "Laz, I'd like to get these cars out of sight of the highway as soon as possible.

We're really not supposed to be here. I'll open up the gate and then we can park in by our new Interpretive Centre before heading further into the park."

"Sounds great," Mac offered, perhaps too quickly. Laz stepped in front of him as Ernie moved off towards the locked gate. "Hey, relax man. I'm old enough to be her father, I know that," Mac stated as he patted his classmate on the shoulder. "I will respect the fact that she is with another guy. However, that should not stop me from being polite. Correct?"

"I'll be watching," Laz reminded him.

"Well, you watch me as I watch the pretty, young lady there having difficulty getting the lock open. Shall I offer to help or do you want to?" Mac offered with his hands spread wide.

"I'll go," was Laz's curt response, as he trod off towards his cousin and the gate.

Within an hour the three were sitting around a small campfire. The soft glow of the fire threw off enough light to illuminate the front of the tiny, two-bedroom log cabin located nearby.

"I loved when the park put these small cabins in for tourists to rent," Ernie said dreamily as she poured herself a glass of her favourite red wine, a merlot from Nk'Mip Cellars, a not too distant Lake Osoyoos, B.C., winery. "The administration gave all park staff a full season to test them out before making them available to the public. I spent all summer out here and I didn't have to drive back and forth between here and Lethbridge once. It was heaven!"

"Are they all in such beautiful locations?" Mac asked, as he looked up into the sky between the coulee walls, never seeing the stars or the moon as bright as right then. It felt surreal.

"To be honest," Ernie began, "I'm kind of biased towards this spot because this is where I stayed this past summer. There are a few more cabins that give gorgeous vistas, almost as good as this one," she finished with a huge grin.

"So, tell us a bit about the park," Laz urged as he handed Ernie the joint he had just finished rolling.

"Well," she began and then flicked on the lighter that accompanied the joint being shared between the three of them, taking a long drag before passing it to Mac. She continued after exhaling. "This past year had been an exciting time actually, at least until they closed us up. We used to think that the prairies didn't begin being occupied until about ten thousand years ago, after the last major ice age. One of our archaeologists, however, thinks she found a Clovis point this past summer. That would **significantly** alter our idea of how long we think Natives have been in the area," Ernie shared, obvious excitement in her voice.

"How so?" asked Mac, as he exhaled a few perfect smoke rings.

"Well, most archaeologists agree that the area around the Milk River was first occupied about ten thousand years ago. A Clovis point, though, suggests the presence of people a couple thousand years before this," Ernie began, as she outlined the shape of a Clovis point on the ground. "Naturally, there are a lot of researchers skeptical because it challenges long-held beliefs. You know, I used to be so naïve about the politics in science. I always thought science was to uncover the truth-"

"The truth? You can't handle the truth!" Mac interrupted.

"What are you talking about?" Laz said, placing his hands out, palms up, pleading for a reasonable explanation.

"Sorry," Mac replied in apology, chuckling a bit. "Sorry, I have to remember that not everybody watches all the movies I do. It's a great line from the late Jack Nicholson in a movie called *A Few Good Men*. He's an army colonel that's defending certain military practices and decisions as 'legitimate' but are of course beyond the understanding of the civilians who take advantage of the freedoms that the military provides for the average Joe, or Jill," he finished, nodding in Ernie's direction.

"You really are a pessimist, aren't you," Ernie stated, as she took a sip of wine.

"No," Mac replied. "I consider myself more of a contrarian, or maybe realist, I don't know."

"Contrarian?" Ernie enquired.

"Yeah, somebody who likes to take up a position that is opposed by the majority." He sat back in his tattered Hockey Canada lawn chair and took a deep breath. "What is the truth? Whose version of the truth should we believe? While our leaders feed us one version, reality on the ground seems to stand in stark contrast. I'll start by asking a simple question; why are we still in the Middle East after all these years? Especially considering all the casualties we've suffered?"

"We're helping to keep the peace while they transition from dictatorships to democracies," Ernie replied, as Laz nodded in agreement.

"Oh, you kids are so naïve," Mac responded. "Please finish filling us in on the importance of this Clovis point and then I'll tell you a tale about a scientist who saw the future and tried to warn humanity. But instead, he and his ideas were ostracised by politicians and his profession alike. At least until history proved him right."

Those who want to face their responsibilities with a genuine commit-
ment to democracy and freedom—even to decent survival—should
recognise the barriers that stand in the way. In violent states these
are not concealed. In more democratic societies barriers are more
subtle. While methods differ sharply from more brutal to more free
societies, the goals are in many ways similar: to ensure the 'great
beast,' as Alexander Hamilton called the people, does not stray from its
proper confines.
Controlling the general population has always been a dominant
concern of power and privilege...
Problems of domestic control become particularly severe when the
governing authorities carry out policies that are opposed by the general
population. In those cases, the political leadership may... manufacture
consent for its murderous policies.

Noam Chomsky, 2003
Hegemony or Survival: America's Quest for Global Dominance

April 3, 5:00 a.m.

Marissa rose from the fire and turned to find her little sister beginning to wake. She went to her sister's side and covered her with the
blanket that had been kicked off. She rubbed Kat's back and began to
sing the lullaby that their mother had enjoyed singing to the girls at
bedtime when each was a toddler.

Tears began to swell in the corners of her eyes and her voice
cracked as she sang. Her parents were gone. They had left one night
and not returned. After four months Marissa still had little idea as to

what had happened to them. She wiped at her eyes and concentrated on trying to settle Kat. She needed to be strong for her sister.

Since the fire would likely burn well past sunrise, Marissa curled up beside her sister on the bed and hugged her tight. The light bounced around the room with the flickering of the flames as Marissa held her sister and hummed. With luck they would be okay for a few more weeks but after that Marissa wasn't sure what they were going to do.

She purposely reviewed the positives. Water was not a problem with the river passing through the back of their property. Food supplies in their cold cellar were running low but would carry them for at least another couple of weeks without going too far below an ideal caloric level. The family had a store of seeds from last year's vegetable garden harvest and some other recently purchased packages of various vegetables to sow. Their young fruit trees should also begin to bear more fruit, but these food sources were months away. Keep positive, she thought.

Some of the problems Marissa and her sister faced loomed before her, too overwhelming to keep locked away for very long. Just the brief thought of realising that the canned goods and other purchased groceries were running low created a burst of adrenaline and she began to shake slightly. Marissa could feel her anxiety heightening and took a couple of slow and deliberate deep breaths. It was impossible to clear her mind and try to sleep. She kept breathing slowly and deeply, rebalancing her body to the natural chemical rush that had caused her shaking.

Okay, analyse the problem and solve it to the best of your ability, she thought. Control what you can control. She needed to think of some way to keep her and her sister fed. Marissa knew that her family's small vegetable garden, as it was, would not keep the two of them fed for much more than a couple of months. She would have to try and increase the size of the garden and plant as much as she could. Then hope for the best.

The planting would be easy but she'd have to clear a lot of sod and brush. Her parents' property had not been prepared for the kind of food production she would have to attempt. She didn't think her eight-year-old sister was going to be able to help with too many physically-demanding tasks but she would find something productive for her to do. Marissa wasn't looking forward to the heavy labour she would have to perform alone. She could think of no other solution to their dilemma, however. With no electricity, storing some of the food they grew might be problematic but she would deal with that later. They needed the food first.

Here she was, in what she still considered an unfamiliar home, with no car. She was continuing to have difficulty coming to terms with her parents having moved out of her childhood home: a home that she knew so well. A home that was secure, that was safe.

Marissa thought that food would be easy compared to what was beginning to gnaw at the back of her thoughts: she was almost out of medication. She could begin to sense some of her darkest fears bubbling near the surface. She didn't know if she could get through this without her meds.

She knew the strategies that she had been taught as a teen inside-out. Nothing, however, could have prepared her for this nightmare they were living. In the middle of nowhere, cut off from everyone, and with no power of any kind. Four months they'd been struggling to stay warm and eat regularly. Spring was quickly approaching but the end of her prescription was charging at her even faster.

Memories from the evening when her parents made their fateful plan began to seep into her thoughts...

"That's it then, we head out tomorrow," Thomas Burke said with more authority than he meant.

"Yes, we've all agreed," his wife, Takara, gently reminded him.

Marissa reluctantly agreed, "I guess."

"Feeling differently now that the challenge is real?" said her father, pushing her a little.

"I just," she started then paused for a moment. "I know. I need to face my anxieties, and I can. Do we have to do this right now? I just got home after a tortuous term. I really need to relax."

"You can't plan these moments," her mother stated. "There are times when we must stand up and speak out against our government. Without a massive protest politicians will continue to ignore our rights, making changes that are against our *Charter*. We've all agreed that this is one of those times. We will be with Aunt Kimiko in Toronto and we will be in touch every day, you know that."

"I know, I know. I just don't know about staying here without you," Marissa replied, feeling her anxiety beginning to surface.

"You and your sister will be fine. Everything you need is here. We should only be gone a couple of days," her father reassured her. "Kat knows the house and property as well as any of us, and will be a great asset, right Kat?"

"I guess, Daddy. But I still don't understand why you have to leave," Kat answered.

"We'll talk about it more when we get back. For now, I think it's important that you know that our leaders have been making changes that your mum and I would call illegal. And, many people across the country agree. We are expecting millions this weekend."

"How can they do it if it's illegal?" Kat asked.

"That's a great question and it's one that they refuse to answer. So, it's not enough that just a few people speak out. Your mum and I need to do our part too," Thomas explained.

"But Dad," Marissa started, and then paused. "I know you and Mum really want to go but I don't know if I can do this right now."

"You'll be fine, Mar," her mother stated, as she reached out and took her oldest daughter's hand. Caressing the back of her daughter's hand, she continued. "You have been away for the entire term and performed wonderfully. I think we only got one panicked phone call the entire time. You are doing so magnificently and we'll be gone for no more than three or four days. It will be a great time to unpack your things and spend a few days relaxing and getting to know your little sister better, and our new home."

"Thanks for the reassurance, Mum," Marissa responded as she removed her hand from her mother's grip and sat back in her chair. "I know I'll be fine. I'm just worried. You know I've never been good with transitions and this one involves a new home."

"Four days, no more," her father reassured her.

…Four days, Marissa thought, right. It had now been almost four months with no word from the outside world at all. All because her parents had decided to go completely retro and move from the suburban home Marissa had grown up in to a log cabin in the middle of nowhere. To make things worse, they had taken the only car!

She had to admit, though, that in a way it was a blessing. If they had still been living in the suburban neighbourhood where she grew up and power had been lost for this long, she and her sister might be doing much worse. Without power at their old home, they would have been without everything they had been depending upon.

They wouldn't have had a large root cellar full of garden vegetables and other food supplies; it had ensured they were able to eat these past four months. They wouldn't have had enough space to grow the plants that could help feed them. Most importantly, there would not have been a river close by with clean, dependable water.

When the radio stations went off the air, however, she was cut off from the outside world completely. Her knowledge of what happened to her parents was limited to some brief news reports and a single phone call from her aunt just before she lost cell contact…

"Hello Aunt Kimiko," Marissa said as she answered her BlackBerry.

"Hi, honey. How are you?" her aunt began.

"Great, except for the fact that Kat keeps beating me at chess!"

"She must get that from her dad because, if I remember correctly, your mother is terrible at chess," her aunt laughed. "Honey, listen, everybody is fine here but we are a little worried."

Marissa could feel her heart start to beat faster. An adrenaline rush caused by a quick burst of anxiety. "What do you mean Aunt Kimmy?"

"Umhh," her aunt began. "Your mum and dad have been caught in a group surrounded by the security here. I know that we were all expecting them to be driving back tomorrow but I can't guarantee that that's going to happen," Aunt Kimiko stated in as reassuring a tone as was possible given the situation.

"What happened?" Marissa stammered.

"Well, security started kettling the protesters just as they did during the G20 in Toronto a few years ago. Do you remember?"

"Yes, I remember. I think there were more than three hundred protesters and bystanders kettled into an area they couldn't leave from. Many were actually just on their way home from work but all of them were forced to stand in the rain for more than four hours. There was, um," she paused to retrieve the facts.

Kettling was a strategy used by police forces worldwide. Large lines or cordons of police, usually in full riot gear or on horseback, would direct large groups into an area that would often have no exit, much like corralling herds of cows or sheep. One of the big controversies about the tactic was that it also ensnares innocent bystanders. After a lot of media coverage following the kettling that the Toronto Police had performed during the 2010 G20 meeting, leaders made a public declaration to never use the approach again.

"Now I recall what I wanted to say," Marissa continued after a short delay. "There was a general counsel from the Civil Liberties Association who argued that the action was against the *Charter of Rights and Freedoms*. Section 9, states that: 'Everyone has the right not to be arbitrarily detained or imprisoned.' That's right; the three hundred were released after four hours without charge. I think the worst example has been with the London Metropolitan Police in England. They used the strategy on disabled persons at a Disability Protest in 1995. The police actually fenced them in like cattle."

"That's my Mar. Always had a great memory. Wish I could remember what happened yesterday," her Aunt comically added. "Anyways, honey, none of us were expecting it and we got separated. Your uncle and I are heading back down to Queen's Park right now. That's where the police have started holding many of the protesters. I'll call you when we find your mum and dad. Love you honey and give Kat a big hug from me."

"Okay, thanks Aunt Kimmy," Marissa replied hesitantly.

"What did Aunt Kimmy want, Mar?" Kat asked immediately after Marissa ended the call.

"Ah," Marissa paused not knowing how much to share with her little sister.

"Just tell me, Mar. I'll find out when Mum and Dad get home anyways. They've told me ALL their protest stories," Kat stated matter-of-factly and with a hint of boredom.

Marissa couldn't help but shake her head as she and her sister were so different. Kat always seemed to be so formal, so mature and had none of the anxieties her sister had. Marissa's heart was pounding and her hands were shaking slightly. She could sense the panic in her voice as she started filling in her sister.

It was only a couple of hours later that she lost her cell connection. It dropped and never came back.

…Thankfully, perhaps, her parents had a couple of radios in the house. She didn't learn what happened to her parents specifically, but what she did learn worried her immensely.

The core of the city had fallen under police and military control. No news was available beyond what the spokesperson for the government was providing. At one point, one of the independent media outlets reported on a leak that the government had shut down all cellular and land communication. The rumour was quickly denied by the government.

For four days all the stations were reporting on the situation in Toronto. During the first night it was observed that many armed forces had moved into the area to reinforce the police against the 'riotous mobs'.

The government announced a state of emergency the next morning. It was reported that a terrorist attack on Queen's Park, centre of the provincial legislature, had taken place. The communication difficulties were being blamed on associated attacks. In order to ensure public safety, the police and armed forces were given powers to arrest and detain within a prescribed 'safety zone'. The solitary news release about the security activity inside the safety zone was that many terrorists had been arrested.

Media analysis consisted of verbatim renderings of the various news releases by the provincial public relations personnel. At the top of each hour, a news release was shared with the media. Using the catchphrase of 'public safety', each news release increased the size of the safety zone and outlined additional search and seizure powers. On the fourth day, the house had lost power and the stations stopped transmitting.

Two days later the power was back on. For some reason, however, Marissa could no longer find any operating radio station except one, CBC. But all she got was the same message over and over: 'This is a broadcast from your provincial and federal governments. A state of emergency has been declared for the entire country. We will advise you of further developments in the coming hours."

Three days later the power was lost again and CBC went dead without the message ever having changed. The power had yet to come back on.

Marissa tried not to think about the worst. She noted that her breathing had quickened again and her heart was pounding. She tried to picture her parents sitting at her aunt's telling stories about their days in university and some of the protests they had been involved in. She thought about them passing around a joint as they chatted, and giggled. During all of this she focused on her breathing, deep and slow, deep and slow. She had her sister to be strong for. That was far more responsibility than she wanted, ever...

"What about a veterinarian?" Thomas asked his oldest daughter at the dinner table.

"You still have to be responsible for an animal's life. I could never anaesthetise anything living, Daddy," replied Marissa.

"You can't avoid responsibility in any job that I know of, honey," he replied as he patted the back of her hand.

"I know that," she replied sullenly. "I just," she paused and looked up at her father. "I'm not good at anything."

"That's not true, Mar," her little sister spoke up. "You know everything there is to know about the Toronto Maple Leafs and the Blue Jays."

Everybody around the table laughed. Marissa was the family's walking encyclopedia about two of Toronto's major sports franchises. When she was four, she had been taken to a baseball game by her father. The next day she had started reading everything she could on the Blue Jays. That fall she started watching some hockey games with her dad and began reading everything she could on the Leafs.

"That is a skill many jobs require!" her mother added, trying to boost Marissa's confidence.

"What? To remember useless sports facts?" Marissa asked sarcastically.

"Not only to be able to recall facts from things you have read or heard, but you're also able to then put together a well-reasoned and informed argument to support an opinion or belief. You excel at that ability, Marissa," her father said and stroked her hair.

"But I only like reading certain things," Marissa said, as she sensed her eyes starting to tear-up.

"Well, let's keep trying new books to read when we go to the library. Let's see if there are more things that appeal to you, honey," her mother suggested.

"What are you reading right now?" her father asked.

"I've started reading about the Theory of Punctuated Equilibrium," Marissa stated proudly.

"The theory of what?" Thomas asked. "Are you studying this for school?"

"Daddy, you know that I don't like anything they make me read at school. Why can't they let me read more of the books I want to read?" Marissa enquired.

This was a perennial question in the Burke household ever since Marissa had started school. She only wanted to read about the Blue Jays and Leafs in kindergarten and grade one. The school had been accommodating Marissa as best it could. After all, she was reading chapter books and novels upon entering kindergarten.

The school had let it go for a few years but once the demands required Marissa to begin reading more widely, especially on topics she wasn't interested in, the emotional meltdowns had begun. The worst had happened in grade four when she wasn't allowed to do a presentation on former U.S. Vice President Dick Cheney's involvement in the attacks that took place on September 11, 2001 in the United States. She had the title already chosen: Was 9/11 another Pearl Harbour?

Marissa continued, "Punctuated Equilibrium, a theory first presented by Stephen Jay Gould and Niles Eldridge in 1972, is the idea that major physical evolution occurs in quick bursts, relatively speaking, rather than in the slow, gradual process of natural selection that Alfred Wallace suggested in 1859. The fossil record shows that species stability is the norm and that this is punctuated by quick periods of speciation when changes take place."

"Fascinating, Marissa, but you're forgetting Charles Darwin, I think," her mother offered.

"Darwin always gets the credit for his insights regarding evolution. Wallace thought up the idea of natural selection independent of Darwin, but rarely gets mentioned," Marissa replied. "Oh, before I forget there's a note in my school bag from my vice principal. I got into another argument with the science teacher today."

"Are we ever going to make it through grade ten?" Thomas asked his wife, taking a deep breath and exhaling slowly.

…Kat shivered and Marissa cuddled in closer to her, hugging her sister's small body into her own and sharing their warmth. In her mind, she looked at the month's calendar, thinking she could probably stretch her medication out for another five or six weeks.

Thank goodness that her parents had always ensured there was a few months supply of her medication around. She had started reducing the dosage two months ago, when she'd given up on hoping that her parents would walk in the door any minute and everything would return to normal.

Five or six weeks she thought, that's not nearly long enough. She'd been feeling some withdrawal symptoms at each drop in her dosage. They were very debilitating at first: body spasms she couldn't control, slurred speech, and sudden bursts of depression or anger. It was getting easier but she was spending a lot of time sleeping, and she could soon no longer afford that.

Kat had been great through it all. Marissa had explained to her little sister what might happen. She remembered how horrible her last transition had been. There would be times when she would curl into a ball and just hold herself, struggling with the rush of emotions. She'd grab handfuls of hair, pulling at her skull, trying to get the 'two sides fighting each other' out of her head. Her mother would rub her back with a reassuring word every once in a while. "It will be okay Mar," her mum would whisper in her ear.

Kat, bless her eight-year-old heart, had done exactly the same for her older sister that first couple of weeks, two months ago.

"Hey, Mar, is it time to get up already?" Kat asked as she rolled over towards her sister, rubbing at her eyes.

Marissa hadn't even noticed that the sun had started to shine rather brightly behind the window blind; she was so lost in thought. "I guess so," she answered. "And it's your turn to make breakfast," she continued, as she began to tickle her sister.

"No, Mar, Mar, Mar," Kat stammered between gasps of air. "Stop, stop, stop, I'm gonna wet myself." Marissa relaxed the hold she had on her sister. "Please don't do that when I've been asleep all night, my bladder's full," Kat finished between slowing gasps.

"Sorry, Kat, couldn't help myself," Marissa said as she began to reach for her sister again.

Kat quickly grabbed a pillow, knocking her sister off balance just long enough to get away and run to the washroom. "You are SO cruel!" she yelled as she ran out of the bedroom.

Marissa laid back down laughing. Gotta keep laughing, she thought to herself. She rolled off the bed and walked over to the bedroom window, pulling the blind aside just a touch to look outside. She fell back in shock. There was a man standing at the edge of the woods looking right at her.

Okay. Relax. Think. He's too far to have seen me, she told herself. But what was she going to do? Was she safe to talk to this person? Would he know what was going on with the power or phones? Or what's been happening in Toronto?

She walked over to the bathroom and knocked on the door, "Kat, are you almost finished?"

"Just washing my hands," Kat answered. She opened the door with her foot as she scrubbed her hands in the bowl of water sitting on the counter. "What's up?"

"Um, there's somebody outside and I don't know how sa-"

"There's somebody here? Is it Mum and Dad?" Kat yelped as she ran for the door.

"No!" Marissa began screaming. She raced after her little sister who had opened the front door and run out to greet whoever lurked at the edge of the woods. But as Marissa began to catch up to her sister, the man began running at the two of them.

...a clear leverage point: growth. Not only population growth, but economic growth. Growth has costs as well as benefits, and we typically don't count the costs—among which are poverty and hunger, environmental destruction and so on—the whole list of problems we are trying to solve with growth! What is needed is much slower growth, very different kinds of growth, and in some cases no growth or negative growth.

The world leaders are correctly fixated on economic growth as the answer to all problems, but they're pushing with all their might in the wrong direction.

...leverage points frequently are not intuitive. Or if they are, we too often use them backward, systematically worsening whatever problems we are trying to solve.

Donella H. Meadows, 2008
Thinking in Systems: A Primer

April 2, 9:00 p.m.

Sam slipped into the woods behind his house and made his way to his well-hidden root cellar. He stepped into the darkened unit and turned on his flashlight. He knew where everything was located by heart; he could do this without light. He really didn't need a lot from the unit, just a few small food items and last minute supplies. He was ready for his trek north in the morning.

Sam had no idea if he'd be back this way again anytime soon, or ever. He glanced around at the remaining supplies. If any of his family made it here in the next few weeks, they would be well supplied for a few months. Most of the food would keep and they could restock and head north, or remain put if they wanted. Sam had made up his mind to go north; at least until he knew more about what was taking place elsewhere in the province, or country.

Sam had to hand it to his father. Joel Gregory had made his children learn a number of basic survival skills while they were growing up. They would certainly come in handy for the next few months, possibly years.

Having given the last of his gasoline to his sister, he'd be hiking to his northern property. It was a large swath of northern bush he'd purchased a few years earlier after removing all his money from his local bank. No longer trusting the banking system. Instead, he invested in a hard asset: land. It would be a long hike but he'd not given a second thought to supplying Susan with fuel: her need was greater than his. With improving weather, he figured it would only take him a couple of weeks to hike the two hundred plus kilometers. Besides, he could always use the exercise, he told himself.

Sam was hoping that his brother, Dave, would have made it here by now. But, Sam thought, he's well aware of how to access both of my places and he's more than capable of making his way north on his own. It was just better to travel with at least one other person, especially given the unrest that had been bubbling and brewing for the past few years across the province.

He paused on his front porch and took in what could be his final nighttime view of the area. What amazed him most was how bright the stars appeared since power was lost in his area. The Milky Way Galaxy was never so vivid against the black background of space. My god, Sam thought, you don't realise how many other suns there are out there some times. It made him think that humans can't be the only ones trying to figure out the meaning of all this, if there was any meaning at all.

He turned and went back into his house. He picked up the checklist for his supplies from his cluttered kitchen table for a second time. He went through the list, checking it against the supplies spread out before him on the oak table, making sure everything was there. He'd go through the list one more time tomorrow morning before leaving, packing his knapsack as he went.

He put the list down and walked into his living room, picking up the latest book he was reading, The Collapse of Complex Societies, from his coffee table. He relaxed down into his well-worn, leather couch in order to finish the book before he went to sleep.

The book was an older one, published in 1988, but he'd just picked it up last fall. It was a treatise by archaeologist Joseph Tainter that attempted to explain how and why complex societies collapse. He found it more than just a little ironic that he had finally found time to read it while his own society appeared to be collapsing around him.

Just before he opened to the last few pages that he had left to read, Sam slipped his summary notes out of the back of the book. He found early on in life that making notes while he was reading forced him to think about the material more thoroughly. He always tried to paraphrase the author's points rather than copy them verbatim, forcing him to think more deeply about the concept being discussed.

Reading over his notes to refresh his memory, he sat back trying to make sense of Tainter's argument so far. The basic premise seemed to be that societies develop as problem-solving organisations. Subsystems within the larger social system expand and contract as they attempt to solve problems for members of society. To support and sustain any system outside of agricultural production, additional energy would need to be used to produce surplus food.

All systems, however, sooner or later encounter stress due to declining marginal returns, a phenomenon that results when more resources are put into a system than the benefits that are gained from the existence of the system. This develops because the solutions arrived at early in a system's existence are the easiest, cheapest, and most accessible. As time passes, solutions become more costly, difficult, and less accessible.

Sam paused for a moment thinking about how this model explained so much of what he had observed the past decade or so, especially around oil use and production where the vast reserves, such as Ghawar in Saudi Arabia, already had all been found and exploited. Now the oil industry was drilling holes in kilometers of ocean water and earth, looking for more oil but at much greater expense—and greater risk to the environment. In addition, it was applauding the melting of Arctic ice to get at possible reserves buried under the north's ocean floors.

He reached by his feet and picked up the beer he had left there when he sat. It was his last one and he had found it hidden on one of the shelves when he was in his root cellar, thinking now is as good a time as any to drink it. He twisted off the cap and took a sip, enjoying the barley taste of this particular brand while he wondered if he'd ever taste beer again. He also made a mental note to read more on Complexity Theory and Systems Thinking if he ever got the chance. Okay, back to his notes.

A society could collapse because of unexpected stress surges that could not be handled by reserves or surpluses. Alternatively, it could abandon complexity as a means of problem solving and return to a simpler sociopolitical structure, experiencing more localised communities and trade. Societies also became more likely to collapse when their economies falter, as this usually lead to tax increases and significant inflation as the elite look for ways to deal with ballooning debt and expenditures. The biggest concern, though, was for societies where most citizens did not or could not provide their own food. These societies experienced significant starvation and chaos when they collapsed.

Okay, not the happiest of scenarios, Sam thought, as he finished reviewing his notes. It was particularly disturbing because the world seemed to be experiencing collapse almost exactly as outlined by Tainter's model. It was as if those in control of world events had created a checklist on how to collapse a global society and then, item-by-item, ensured that they happened. Virtually every point that Tainter made about a society on the edge of collapse appeared to fit the facts of today's world, at least as Sam understood them.

"Boy, and this was written more than twenty-five years ago," Sam said out loud. He found it exceedingly frustrating that governments had been warned for decades about the endgame of exponential growth but had chosen to ignore the arguments of the scientists and their supporting facts. Instead of standing back and taking in the big picture, leaders had pushed for more growth to profit from short-term expansion. They were pushing the issue that was causing all the problems in the first place!

Ever-increasing investment had to be made in the area of resource extraction. Agricultural soil was showing signs of stress from years of fossil fuel-based fertilizers, pesticides, and herbicides. Environmental catastrophes were becoming more frequent and larger in nature. Global population was growing exponentially. Stress from both external and internal unrest was multiplying everywhere. Currency and trade wars were increasing in severity. More and more citizens were opting for simpler solutions rather than further complexity, stressing sociopolitical organisation and control. The elite were con-solidating power and privilege through economic manipulation and military might. Economies were experiencing debt-based stress like never before.

It was time to see what insights Tainter had for modern society as he saw it over twenty-five years ago. Sam opened the book at the spot indicated by the folded page, took another sip of beer, and resettled himself in the corner of his couch.

Over the next few minutes of reading Sam learned that Tainter didn't believe collapse was possible in today's globalised world because a contemporary society would simply absorb a collaps-ing one.

Interesting thesis, Sam thought as he put the book down. He hadn't yet decided if this book would make the trip north with him. Copies of his favourite books were at both his homes but like this one, a number he had just picked up within the last year. He would take about half a dozen of his newest books and Tainter's would likely be one of them. He'd decide in the morning. And, if things got really desperate, he could burn them for fuel or use them for toilet paper.

As he stood up and stretched his back, he took the final few sips of this his last beer. Probably not the best thing to be reading just before he headed off to bed, he reflected. However, he had wanted to finish it before he began his trek tomorrow.

He walked around the house one last time to make sure everything was secure. He had little of real value in either house except his books. He did want to ensure, however, that it was capable of providing shelter and supplies for at least one member of his family, if they ever made it here.

In a world of modern finance, you don't have to live in Europe to be touched by what happens in Athens or Madrid, anymore than you needed to own a home in Cleveland to feel the collapse of the subprime mortgage market. Thanks to our integrated global banking system, a financial market accident in one corner of the world now puts everyone at risk. An investment arm of your local bank could be exposed to a French bank, which in turn hold a big position in Greek bonds that are about to go horribly offside. When that happens, the pain ripples from Greece's bond market, to the French bank, to your regional investment dealer, and eventually your doorstep. Half a world away, you and millions of other depositors have a direct interest in Greek debt, even though none of you personally have invested a penny in Greece.

Jeff Rubin, 2012
The End of Growth

December 12, 3:00 p.m.

"Wow! I'm at a loss for words-" Ranjeet began and then, thinking quickly, paused, put the box down and embraced his wife, holding her tightly. While he was excited about having a child he couldn't help but feel some dread considering what Mike had just shared with him, and where it had taken his thoughts.

Hoping Mike was wrong but knowing, deep inside, that there was more going on here than just a one-day bank closure to implement a stress-test, he slid his hands down to Chandra's hips, moved her back slightly so he could see her face and made a suggestion. "I know you don't like to skip classes and you just missed today because of the doctor's appointment, but how about you take tomorrow off and we celebrate with a quick get-away for the weekend. I have an extra day and we can head out of town. I can pamper my new mother-to-be and we can avoid the chaos from the protest planned for Toronto this weekend. What do you say?"

"I thought being pregnant was shocking," she replied with awe. "Are you being romantic Mr. Saini? I should be pregnant more often, yes?"

"Let's get through the first one, shall we?" Ranjeet replied, his mind racing. "It's still early, so let's head out as soon as we can. Just pack a couple of day bags with enough to get us both by for two or three days, okay. I've got to run down to the storage unit for something, but I'll be right back. I love you," he ended as he leaned in, grasped his wife's head using both hands and brought her close for an intimate kiss.

"Oh, this could be a **very** exciting weekend. I just got some new lingerie from Victoria's Secret," she replied as she took his hands in hers and moved them down to her hips again, stepping closer and moving seductively against him.

"It's working, keep talking," he said, as he slowly moved his hands backwards from her hips and pulled her tighter for a moment. He relaxed his grip and kissed her deeply again.

"I'd better start packing or we're never going to get out of here," she interrupted as Ranjeet's hands had begun to creep under her top. "You go get what you need from the storage unit and I'll get our stuff together. Dad!" she added as she moved away from him.

"Don't know if I'm going to get used to that," he replied smiling.

"Well, you've got a few months to get used to it. We couldn't have bought a house at a better time. Thank goodness it's almost done. You run, I'll get ready. I love you so much!" Chandra responded, as she literally skipped off towards the bedroom.

As soon as he had closed the door to their unit Ranjeet took a deep breath and leaned against the hallway wall. What perfect timing, he thought, somewhat sarcastically, as his anxiety about the banking situation grew. He brought his hands up to his head and ran his fingers back and forth in his short, black hair. He massaged his scalp a bit, trying to relieve some of the building tension. God, I hope Mike's wrong, he thought. Pushing himself off the wall he turned towards the stairs and began walking.

The door to the stairs opened just before he arrived and his neighbour, Kim, walked out.

"Hey, Kim, how are you?" Ranjeet greeted her.

"After carrying a couple of bags of groceries up twenty-three flights of stairs? Exhausted! How about you Ranjeet? Have you and Chandra thought about joining us?" she asked as she placed the grocery bags down, shaking out her arms and massaging her shoulders.

"We really appreciate the offer but we're going to head out of town for a couple of days. I've got tomorrow off and-" Ranjeet began.

"Long weekend, huh?" Kim interrupted and then enthusiastically continued. "Nice, well as always you and Chandra are more than welcome to come along. Nothing like a good political protest to get the old adrenaline pumping! My sister and her husband are joining us from up north. Look for us on TV," Kim finished as she opened her unit door and walked in.

This is a good time to leave the downtown core, thought Ranjeet. The Occupiers had called for massive protests this weekend in five major centres across the country: Ottawa, Vancouver, Calgary, Montreal, and Toronto.

When the news hits the wires about the banks it could create even more animosity between the powerful banking industry and government, and the protest movement. Tension had been growing globally between citizens and their governments and banks since the Arab Spring.

Ranjeet met several other residents of his condominium complex on the way down the stairs. He didn't know many, but as each passed he wondered if they had any idea of what might be coming. He reached the sub-basement where the storage units were located and headed towards his and Chandra's.

It took him about fifteen minutes of moving items around before he found the box he wanted, inside an old sports bag. After quickly checking the contents he placed it back in the sports bag, zipped up the bag and slung it over his shoulder. It was heavier than he remembered, but that was a good thing. He locked up the storage unit and headed back up the stairs.

It took a slow and steady pace, and he made it back to his condo faster than he thought he would. "Have you packed?" he asked Chandra as he shut the door.

"Do we need clothes?" she asked playfully.

"Well," he paused looking at her. "You are a MILF now."

"Oh! You are terrible, Mr. Saini. No sex for you, one year," she teased him, while pointing at him accusingly.

"Yeah, like you could last that long," he replied, his eyebrows rising.

"A lot longer than you, my friend," she said as she moved past him. She managed to stroke his groin on the way by. "The other pack is in the bedroom."

"Just a few overnight items, right?" Ranjeet asked as he hefted the other bag Chandra had packed. "Feels like more than a few."

"Oh, well there are also a couple of books I wanted to read. You know like, What to Expect When You're Expecting and-"

"Didn't you just find out?" Ranjeet asked, a bit confused.

"Yes but Kim next door had the book so she lent it to me and-"

"Kim knew before me?" Ranjeet asked, trying not to sound too accusatory, as he picked up the water and papers he had left by the front door when he had embraced his wife soon after arriving home. He placed Mike's papers inside the sports bag before slinging it over his shoulder again and slipped the water into his jacket pocket.

"No, no, honey. She lent it to me a couple of weeks ago when we started talking about this whole," she paused. "This whole, beginning a family thing," Chandra stated as she opened their unit door and held it open for her husband.

"Yes, I remember talking about starting to think about it, but I didn't expect a result so soon. It's only been a few weeks," Ranjeet replied as he locked the door to their unit.

"You know, both my sisters got pregnant early during their first attempts so it was highly likely-" Chandra responded as she opened the door to the stairs for them both.

"You never told me that," Ranjeet interrupted, as he began down the stairs.

"Why would I tell you something like that Ranj?" she asked rhetorically, looking at him. "And, why on earth are you sweating so much, honey?"

"Probably because I'm going to have a cardiac arrest any moment from going up and down stairs all afternoon," he panted, doing his best Monty Python imitation.

"Do we need to stop?" she responded with some concern in her voice.

"No, I'm okay. Let's keep going. It's actually my stomach that's upset more than anything. We've not got far to go, only," he paused as he looked at the door they were just passing. "Excellent, only another twenty-one stories to go, no problem, me man, me strong!" he announced, pounding his chest with his free hand.

"Oh, Tarzan," Chandra purred. "I like that."

"Let's get out of town, then we can take care of our animal passions, okay?"

"Depends who's driving," she asked as she raised an eyebrow and brought a finger up to her mouth, licking the tip.

"You know what, honey," he started, not wanting to break the mood but needing to share some of the thoughts racing through his mind. "Um, I love you so much, and, um, before, ah-"

"What's up Ranj? You usually play along so well. It sounds like you're going to tell me it's the end of the world or something," Chandra asked raising an eyebrow.

He forced himself to laugh. "No, no. Um, I just have some troubling thoughts regarding today's bank announcement and I thought you could help me work through them. You know, you could be my sounding board."

"As long as I get to hold the mike," she teased. "Of course, honey. We can chat but I just might have my mouth full and-"

"You are so bad, woman," he interrupted. "You know a child will put a crimp in our lifestyle."

"I know," she replied sullenly. "I've been thinking about that a little. I want a child, but I also don't want to miss our time together. Who knows what life will be like after a baby arrives? Everything will be different. It won't just be you and me anymore," she paused. "It will be you and me and a little, me-you," she said as she struggled to find a word that would suit. "I think I like me-you better than you-me. It sounds better, don't you think?"

"Is this the name we're going with then? Mee-Yew?" Ranjeet replied, trying to imitate his grandfather. "It doesn't sound Hindi to me. It sounds like a hungry cat."

Chandra giggled, "No, silly. I'm just be-" Chandra was interrupted by Ranjeet's phone ringing.

"I'm sorry, honey," Ranjeet apologized. "I am expecting an important phone call so just let me take this," he explained, as he stopped descending the stairs and pulled his phone out of his jacket pocket.

Chandra continued down a few more stairs then stopped to wait for her husband.

"That's fantastic, thank you," Ranjeet concluded. He ended the call and placed his phone back in his jacket, smiling as he began down the stairs towards his wife.

"I've arranged to stay at a bed and breakfast up north this weekend and-" Ranjeet began.

"Oh, do you remember the little B&B right beside the house we're having built," Chandra interrupted. "It was so pretty. Will it be something like that?" she asked.

"Well, actually, it is the one beside our soon-to-be-home. That call was the confirmation. We were lucky they had a cancellation yesterday, so we have the last available room."

"Oh my god, Ranj. That's wonderful!" she replied, grinning from ear-to-ear.

They got to the car and put everything they were carrying in the trunk except for Chandra's oversized purse, which she placed by her feet. Ranjeet hoped that they would be able to head back home on Sunday but it might all depend on what the banks did.

"What would you like to listen to?" he asked his wife as she slid into the passenger seat.

"How about some reggae, I'm in the mood for a little Bob Marley."

"Any particular song?" Ranjeet asked.

"I really like 'Three Little Birds'. It's on his *Exodus* album."

Ranjeet hit the steering wheel control buttons for his car's stereo system. It took him a moment to remember the exact order since he hadn't driven his car for well over a month; gas was just too damn expensive. He was glad that their new home was within walking distance of public transit otherwise they would not have been able to move there and afford for him to commute back and forth. The benefit of living in the city was that it certainly had better public transportation options than more rural and suburban areas.

"Play 'Three Little Birds'," he said to the voice-controlled system when prompted. The music began softly in the background as Ranjeet turned the corner and headed up from the parking level. Although it was still relatively early on Thursday, and the real protest wasn't supposed to begin until tomorrow evening, there was a large security presence already. The security preparations provided a stark contrast to the chorus of Bob Marley's 'Three Little Birds' playing softly in the background as they drove out onto Toronto's streets—

Don't worry about a thing, 'cause every little thing gonna be alright.

Singing don't worry about a thing, 'cause every little thing gonna be alright.

"Boy, these guys are looking pretty serious," Chandra said as they began driving down the street. "I haven't seen this much security out, ever. Not even after Anonymous successfully shut down NORAD for a weekend."

"They've obviously brought in reinforcements," Ranjeet responded, as surprised as his wife at the security presence already.

As they turned another corner they came upon a number of flat bed trucks parked along the roadside. Half a dozen forklifts were being employed to unload cement-based barrier fences and place them along the curb. But in some places they were actually closing off access to streets completely.

Ranjeet and Chandra didn't do lot of talking as they were both stunned by the preparations of the police. Occasionally they would point out to each other more and more signs of security mobilisation throughout the core. They also saw cordons of forces around public buildings and banks.

It took them an extra hour to get out of the city core, then another hour to make it to the highway ramp. As soon as they were cruising smoothly along one of Greater Toronto Area's main north-south routes, Highway 404, they relaxed.

"Boy, I've never seen it like that before. I thought the last Occupier protest was bad. I think there may be more security personnel than protesters tomorrow. I'm glad you suggested we head out this weekend," Chandra stated with concern peppered in her voice. "How are you feeling?"

"I've got a bit of a chill and my stomach cramps are a bit bothersome, but I'm sure it's all the climbing I've been doing today. Or maybe I've got a bit of the flu coming on. Nothing serious, I'm sure," Ranjeet assured his wife, although the stomach cramps were beginning to remind him of those he had suffered through during their honeymoon in Cancun, Mexico when he had succumbed to Montezuma's Revenge for most of their stay. It had turned out to be the least romantic of vacations.

"Maybe," Chandra responded. "Hey, you seemed pretty animated about wanting to talk about something before we left. Want to start?"

"Sure. You know I've got tomorrow off but you don't know why," Ranjeet began. "The banks are being closed by the government," he glanced at the car's clock. "In fact, the announcement will be made in just a few minutes, at seven o'clock. We've been told that they want to perform another stress-test and check our capitalisation, but I'm worried," Ranjeet explained, his voice betraying his increasing discomfort with the situation.

"That's why you sent me the text?" Chandra asked. "Because you're worried?"

"Yes, you took it all out right?" Ranjeet asked in return.

"Yeah," Chandra confirmed. "I took everything out of our savings and chequing accounts, and the safety deposit box as you asked. There wasn't a lot of cash, but it's in my purse. Why do we need the cash, anyways?"

"I'm not a hundred percent sure about what's going to happen next week with the banks but I'll try to explain. Um, but I need to step back a bit and talk about money and its role in society for it to make sense, okay?" he asked, glancing at his wife for a brief moment.

"Sure, honey," Chandra replied, stroking his right forearm.

"Okay, so economic textbooks tend to view money as having three purposes. First, it is a medium of exchange. You give me something I want or need and I'll give you some money. The money I gave you can then be used to make an exchange by you for something else from someone else and so on. We can do this because it has an agreed-upon value."

"Okay," Chandra said, indicating her understanding.

"Second, it is supposed to be a store of value. It should hold its purchasing power over time. This allows savers to put off some spending for a future date, assuming that their money won't be of lesser value.

"Third, it is the standard value that provides an agreed-upon measurement of the cost of goods and/or services."

"I think I follow you so far," Chandra stated, continuing to acknowledge she was listening to her husband.

"But," Ranjeet emphasised, "when you drill right down to the bedrock of money you realise it's a completely human construct based purely on trust. I'll give you my money and in exchange you'll give me a product or service. Then that money that I give you can be used to purchase another service or product since society agrees that a piece of paper, or coin, or whatever, is of value and thereby exchangeable."

"I understand," Chandra acknowledged, while observing that the traffic heading into Toronto on the opposing highway lanes was completely stopped. In fact, many drivers were standing outside their cars talking on cell phones or with someone close by. "But don't we use paper money instead of having to barter with home-grown food and such, as in times past?" Chandra offered.

"Yeah, you're partially right if we go far enough back in economic history, but if we look at today's environment money acts as a medium of exchange and an agreed-upon measurement of value, but it sure doesn't hold its value well at all. Inflation eats away at its value every day and remember inflation is purposely sought by the world's central banks. They deplore deflation as it causes their bread and butter, debt, to contract.

"Now, at one time our money did hold its value, sort of; when money was made from gold and/or silver. Periods of inflation still existed, but they were usually balanced out by times of deflation, when prices fell. So over the long run you would encounter little in the way of inflation. This was primarily because there was a **fixed** amount of gold and silver circulating as money."

"So, why don't we still have gold or silver in our coins?" Chandra asked, noticing that her husband's colour was off and thinking that he was obviously fighting something.

Ranjeet paused and took the bottle of water he had brought with him out of his jacket pocket. He was really thirsty for some reason so he took a long sip and then continued. "That's a great question, honey, and part of the answer is what the money creators discovered thousands of years ago.

"Early on in the story of money it was discovered that those in charge of money could expand the amount of money they had in several ways. The Romans, for example, began to make their coins smaller and/or reduced the amount of precious metals in the coins.

Our government did the same in the late 1960s when they removed silver content from our dimes and quarters.

"Nowadays, all a country's central bank has to do is push a button to create some more zeroes on a balance sheet and, voila, we have many billions or a trillion more dollars floating around in the system.

"In fact, for the past few years many of the globe's central banks have been pouring more and more fiat currency into the system. There are now literally hundreds of trillions of dollars, pounds, yen, and every currency possible, in IOUs floating around the globe. The largest portion of these IOUs has been written by the world's developed economies, like Canada. Some observers put G10 debt at over $900 Trillion when everything is counted."

"Shouldn't more money within the system getting spent improve the economy?" Chandra asked, beginning to have some difficulty understanding the direction her husband's conversation was heading.

"It's not quite as simple as that," Ranjeet answered. "What I'm finally realizing, though, is that it is solely confidence in continued growth that is holding this all together. Mike has helped me realise that our leadersh-" Ranjeet was saying when Chandra interrupted.

"Ranj, you were talking to Mike. Oh god, what is the conspiracy this time?" Chandra asked putting her head back on the seat's headrest.

"Honey, I admit he's a bit obsessed about conspiracy theories but he's a brilliant guy," Ranjeet offered in defense.

"He's crazy, that's what he is," Chandra countered, shaking her head.

"Yes he's crazy, but so was Einstein from what I've heard. Just let me finish because it seems to be coming together for me a little as I talk about it. Please, Chandra, just humour me for a little while longer."

"Okay but this is killing my libido," she teased him, as she stroked him with her left hand.

"Don't make me stop this car young lady," he warned her, while shaking a finger in her direction.

She removed her hand, crossing her fingers with those from her other hand, and placed both hands in her lap. "I will behave until we get to the B&B. Promise," she stated. "But your fly is undone. You might want to fix that before we get out of the car and greet anyone," she giggled.

"I don't know how you did that so fast or unnoticed, but good work. Anyways, where was I? Oh, yes, confidence. The economic system is all about confidence. And our leaders will say anything to maintain that confidence. They will lie and lie and continue to lie some more, even when the truth has become obvious to everyone. They will not admit to any problems or mistakes because once confidence in the system is lost, the system collapses. It is that fragile," he asserted, more to himself than to his wife.

Some of these thoughts had been playing in the background of his mind ever since being moved from his branch to the head office. He was now having to follow the daily action of the banking industry on a global level, rather than dealing with customers and providing financial advice in a small local branch. Mike's push helped Ranjeet to consolidate some of the disparate thoughts that had been circulating in his head.

"Why is this so important right now?" he continued. "Well, it's because of the fractional reserve system that our banks use. When the subprime mortgage fiasco led to the bankruptcies of some big players, like AIG Insurance and Lehman Brothers, regulations to prevent such excessive leverage were supposed to have been put in place."

"Did the regulations not help?" Chandra asked.

"No, because none of that has happened. The situation is actually worse than when the crisis started. The financial institutions have leveraged their assets so many times over that if people lose confidence and begin to take their cash or assets out of the system, the entire structure is going to fall apart. And it isn't going to take much because it appears that we're on the razor's edge.

"I should have seen this ages ago but I've finally come to realise that the entire fiat currency system is basically a Ponzi scheme," Ranj concluded emphatically

"Ponzi scheme? Okay that's a new one for me. Do you mean pyramid scheme?" Chandra asked, having heard the term pyramid scheme in some other context that she couldn't immediately recall.

"Yes, a pyramid scheme is another name for a Ponzi scheme," Ranjeet replied to his wife's question. "The term Ponzi comes from Charles Ponzi, who in the early 1900s used the attraction of high rates of return on investments to steal almost half a million dollars—about six million in today's dollars.

"The scheme wasn't invented by Ponzi though. He actually learned it while working for a bank in Montreal. There's our Canadian content for the scheme," Ranjeet noted. "The bank was offering higher interest rates than everywhere else at the time and it was only able to do this because it was funding its rate through the deposits of new customers.

"Such a scheme can only continue if new deposits keep coming in. Once new customers stopped depositing money, the store of funds to pay interest dried up. The pyramid, or Ponzi, collapsed," Ranjeet explained, using one hand to imitate a system collapsing as best he could.

"You may have heard about the biggest case a number of years ago. An investment advisor down in the States, by the name of Bernie Madoff, devised a scheme that has been classified as the biggest ever. Losses were estimated to have been over sixty-five billion dollars at the time. The kicker for the banking industry, however, was that the bank JP Morgan made over a billion dollars through Madoff," Ranjeet added incredulously. "Kind of like they did when MF Global and Peregrine Financial Group went bankrupt a few years ago," he continued.

"I've heard of JP Morgan. They were the ones that went bankrupt just a few weeks ago, but not the other two." Chandra interjected.

"Ah, they were the canaries in the coalmine that should have tipped everyone off to the problems. MFG was an investment firm run by former New York governor and Goldman Sachs executive director, Jon Corzine. It was only the eighth largest American bankruptcy. It's better known, though, for the precedent it set in allowing these large financial institutions to begin stealing client money."

"What? How can that be?" Chandra asked in amazement. She was still attempting to understand Ranjeet's profession and industry.

"Well, client money is supposed to be put into segregated accounts. These accounts are meant to keep client money safe and secure," Ranjeet tried to explain.

"To make a long story short, they took the money out of these segregated accounts, made payouts to some of their banking friends, such as JP Morgan, and then declared bankruptcy. The farmers and teachers and other groups who had money with MFG and PFG were left out in the cold with nothing."

Ranjeet had to stop for a moment as he still wasn't feeling well and began shivering. He continued after taking another sip of water. "Anyways, during Congressional hearings, everyone from MFG, including Corzine, stated that they had no idea where the money went to or what happened to it, that it had 'vapourised'. Some critics started referring to this type of institutional theft as being 'Corzined', if you can imagine. But it did set a precedent and soon other similar institutions were vapourising their clients' money, just like PFG did a few months after the MFG fiasco. The frustrating aspect of these events for a lot of people is that no one at these firms has been charged with anything," Ranjeet lamented, shaking his head slowly.

"So, today all the bank staff are told that, given the chaos in other countries' banking systems, our banks are being closed tonight so that the central bank and government can complete their most comprehensive stress-test yet. But the more I think about things, the more worried I'm getting.

"I'm wondering, if like Mike suggested, they may not open again on Monday or anytime soon. If they're as undercapitalised as pretty well every other bank in the world, we could be in trouble."

"I'm still not sure I understand, honey. Why would banks be so undercapitalised? That means they don't have enough assets to cover their liabilities, right?" Chandra asked, as she took a thermos out of the bag by her feet on the car floor and had a drink. She noted that despite the fact it was the middle of December there were still some flowers in late bloom along the side of the highway. Although she loved the balmy weather, it was worrying that temperatures were so far above normal almost all the time now. Ranjeet's answer to her question brought her focus back to the conversation.

"Yes, you're absolutely right. Okay, consider the fact that the way our economic system is contrived it must have inflation to survive. As a result, our central bank aims to have an inflation rate somewhere between one and three percent. Why? Well, a cynic could argue that inflation serves to keep the scheme from collapsing. The economic system requires growth, and the banks require debt.

"We've been able to grow over the past several hundred years, especially the last couple of hundred, for any number of reasons but particularly because of cheap, untapped resources and population increase.

"However, for the past fifty years or so we've been growing for a different reason. We've been growing because of an increase in debt. Everybody's using debt to purchase items rather than saving until one can actually afford to purchase something. We're using tomorrow's money—which may or may not be there—to consume today.

"Canadian households, for example, have reached their highest debt levels to income in history just recently. We have grown our economy through debt rather than through productive industries and services. I think we have finally encountered our own currency crisis because of all this debt. Our dollar may be witnessing its final swan song with every other fiat currency as the Ponzi begins collapsing. We should be able to use our cash for a while yet, I hope," he finished, pausing and looking over at his wife.

"Wow, quite the tale," she said returning his look and raising her eyebrows. "And you got this all from Mike?"

"No actually. Mike did tell me some political tales that may or may not be true. Who really knows anymore, right? No, what Mike told me is separate from my thinking about how our economic system and the banking industry feed off each other. His stories just gave me a little push towards thinking a bit more skeptically about the system and what the banks have been doing. It was only Mike's reminder to me about the U.S. possibly losing their reserve status that got me thinking."

"Reserve status?" Chandra asked, looking at her husband.

"Okay here's the turnoff, we're almost there," Ranjeet stated as he put on his turn signal and began drifting into the turning lane, touching the brakes to give him manual speed control again. He slowed down and prepared to make the turn towards their new community. "Enough of world economic problems, okay," Ranjeet stated.

"Of course, if you're done talking about it you know I won't bring it up," Chandra responded. "You know, it's too bad the house isn't finished. We could have a second honeymoon," she offered.

"I don't know honey the weather's supposed to be nice. I would like to spend some time outside this time," Ranjeet offered, emphasising outside, as he winked at his wife.

"You're no fun," she teased him back.

"Okay, here is our street," Ranjeet pointed out as he slowed the car even more.

"Oh, I can't wait to see," Chandra gushed, clapping her hands together in excitement.

They approached their new home very slowly. The wooded lot had been partially cleared to make room for the construction. The foundation had been poured and the basic frame was standing. A lot more had been completed since their drive by the property six weeks ago, soon after signing the purchase agreement.

"Looking good," Ranjeet said as the car crept by. "We'll walk over tomorrow and have a closer look, okay."

"Deal," Chandra responded, beside herself with sheer delight.

They continued around the corner to the bed and breakfast next to their property. Chandra grabbed the bag by her feet as they both got out of the car.

Ranjeet opened the trunk giving his wife access to her overnight bag while he took the other one and his sports bag. "What's in the bag?" Chandra asked.

"I'll show you inside," Ranjeet quickly answered as they approached the front door. "It's an emergency money kit of kinds."

Chandra proceeded to knock on the door just as Ranjeet doubled over from severe intestinal pain.

If we have been lied to about mortgages, 401(k)s, stock portfolios, hedge funds, derivatives, insider trading, Ponzi schemes, appraised values, credit ratings, and adjustable rates; if we've been lied to by Bear Stearns and Lehman Brothers, AIG and Citigroup, Bernie Madoff and Standford Financial; if we were lied to about the invasion of Iraq and torture; even about steroids in baseball—then why do so many accept on faith everything we have been sold about energy? Why accept it, especially when the people telling us about energy are the same folks who lied to us about everything else?

Michael Ruppert, 2008
Collapse: Confronting Peak Oil and Money in a Post Peak Oil World

October 15, 9:00 p.m.

The fire had burned down to a pile of red-hot embers in the bottom of the fire pit as Ernie finished her thoughts on the Clovis point and what it meant for regional archaeology. Mac and she had both huddled in a bit closer to the fire in order to keep warm as the temperature had begun to drop rapidly. Laz was busy examining the cameras that he had retrieved from the car. He wanted to make sure they were prepped and ready to go for the morning.

"So, let me tell you about this scientist who predicted the energy crisis over sixty years ago," Mac finally bellowed after a few moments of silence.

"Hang on," Laz urged. He picked up the video camera and flicked on the record button. He wanted to test the settings and thought he could play around while he was filming Mac speak.

Mac took a short sip of his beer, crossed his legs, and leaned back in his chair. "Marion King Hubbert made his biggest contribution to science and the world while he was a geophysicist with Shell Oil. He started working for them during the Second World War. Hubbert was," Mac paused, thinking of the appropriate word. "Um, he was prophetic in his view of the future.

"Using simple oil well production data he predicted the energy dilemma long before anybody was even thinking about it. In fact, it was just after World War Two. Everyone was celebrating the end of the war and saw the future as open to endless possibilities. Nobody but Hubbert was talking about running out of the world's most important resource, petroleum.

"About ten years after the war, Hubbert presented a paper to the American Petroleum Institute in which he argued that the U.S. would hit its peak in oil production in the early-1970s. Because his prediction ran counter to the prevailing view, his argument was dismissed and he was criticized widely within his profession."

He looked directly at Ernie, "You know, like your archaeologist finding a Clovis point, this is one of those unfortunate costs when you challenge the status quo. Facts rarely make a difference to belief systems." He paused for a moment to take a sip of his drink mumbling, "I know," into his beer. Neither of his companions caught his comment.

The moon continued to shine brightly, creating shadows all along the coulee walls. The waning campfire light added to the distortions. The fire began to sputter its last few sparks into the air as Mac began his history lesson. Ernie sat back relaxed, sipping on her drink while Laz played with the settings on the video camera, recording Mac as he became more animated with each word, beginning to speak as much with his hands as his voice.

"Anyways," Mac continued after a moment's reflection, "Hubbert actually laid the foundation for all his later thoughts on what has become known as 'Peak Oil' during his early work on mineral deposits. It was at this time he recognised that the flow of minerals was one way, from a high concentration of ore to being eventually dispersed throughout the world and never to be useful again. In other words, mineral resources could become exhausted. This seems obvious to us today but at the time such thinking was not common. Everyone assumed our resources would last forever," he stressed, as he spread his arms wide.

"He also argued that the start of the flow-line—so the rate of discovery of the resource—had to at least meet the rate of exhaustion of the resource at the end of the flow-line. It is the only way to maintain the flow out of the stock at a steady rate. If the rate of discovery dropped but the flow remained constant, then the stock of resources would eventually run out.

"Or, if the rate of discovery remained constant but the rate of use increased, then the stock would also eventually run out. You see it's all about systems and feedback loops and the timing of delays," Mac intoned as he moved his hands and arms all about him in motions attempting to show the way the system might look and interact.

Ernie began giggling. "You look like a wizard about to cast a spell. Especially the way the moon is casting shadows onto the coulee walls. It's all very," she paused. "Psychedelic. You didn't happen to bring any chocolate, did you Laz?" she asked rolling her head slowly towards him and raising her eyebrows.

Laz reached into his knapsack and threw her a bag. She opened it up, looked inside, and then reached in pulling out a Kit Kat bar. "I love you," she said, blowing a kiss towards her cousin. He just smiled in return.

Mac reached down and picked up a stick lying close to his feet. He began poking the remaining few embers of the fire, sending a burst of sparks into the cool night air.

"So, Hubbert saw that mineral resources would follow a definitive life cycle, with an end. After all, we live on a planet with finite resources, right?" Laz and Ernie both nodded as Laz passed a newly rolled joint to Ernie. "He goes on to work for Shell and it didn't take him long to notice that individual oil fields followed a pattern of production similar to a bell curve. Their production increased exponentially during the early phase, hit a peak, then fell off quickly until the well became unproductive," Mac continued as he leaned further forward and used the stick he had in his hand to draw the Hubbert Curve in the dirt by Ernie's and Laz's feet.

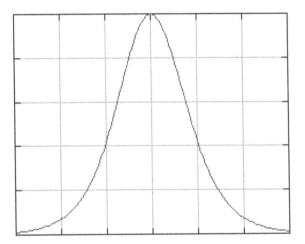

"Now, by unproductive I mean the cost of getting a barrel of oil out of the ground becomes more than it can be sold for—a very important concept known as energy on return of investment, or E.O.R.O.I.," Mac stressed, jabbing the fire as he spelled out the acronym.

"Hubbert had actually been talking about the concept of Peak Oil for a few years before he made that speech to the API, in 1956. He had given presentations and published some articles. His first talk on the subject was actually in 1948, this was followed up by a research article that was published in the journal Science and entitled 'Energy from Fossil Fuels'," Mac continued as he took the joint from Ernie and inhaled deeply, setting his head back and looking up at the stars as he exhaled.

"Okay, I got the munchies now. Anybody want some-" he began, then stopped abruptly as he stood and moved towards the cooler he had packed full of food. "Ah, here it is," he said as he reached down and pulled out a package. He walked over to his lawn chair, sat back down, opened the package and offered Laz and Ernie some home-made sushi.

"Did you make these?" asked Ernie, looking at Mac with a hint of disbelief.

"You bet, and they're all vegetarian, if anybody needs to know," Mac replied.

"Okay, where was I again?" Mac asked, searching his foggy brain for what he had said only moments before.

"You're stoned," giggled Ernie, as she took a final sip of her wine. She turned towards Laz and tipped her glass upside down, showing it was empty. She smiled at him as he picked up the bottle by his feet and began to fill her glass. "Only half Laz, we're scheduled to start early in the morning," she reminded them.

"You were about to talk about a paper Hubbert wrote on fossil fuel energy or something," Laz offered to Mac seeing that he still couldn't recall what he had been discussing.

"It's as bad as playing euchre and never remembering who dealt. Okay, so MK writes this paper in 1949 that specifically outlines the energy dilemma as it applies to petroleum or oil.

"He spells out more than **sixty years ago** the following argument," Mac continued, his voice rising in emphatic tones. "First, the base energy for life on the planet is solar and humans have relied on this solar energy for tens of thousands of years. He further argues that this limited energy input had kept the population of the species in check, not allowing it to grow too quickly.

"However, sometime during the thirteenth century, a group of Britons discovered that black rocks they had found could burn and give off greater energy than the wood they were used to burning.

Mining of this coal eventually led to the smelting of metals and the creation of the steam engine. The steam engine was soon put to use propelling locomotives and large steamships," Mac paused as he noticed Ernie lay her head back and close her eyes. "Are you still with us young lady?"

"Yeah, yeah," she answered quickly. "I just find that the canyon is beginning to spin a little."

"Um, maybe we should put our drinks down and have some water," Mac suggested. He got up, removed the glass from Ernie's hand and dumped out the remaining wine. Setting the glass aside, he grabbed the two remaining canteens he had packed and handed one to Ernie. "Laz, make sure she finishes her canteen of water before she falls asleep. She'll feel better in the morning."

"Sure," Laz replied. "No more smoke for her either. Hey, are you gonna finish your story? I'm starting to get interested," Laz added.

"Well, that makes one of you," Mac smiled as he glanced at Ernie. "Sure, Laz, I just wanna make sure our tour guide here can actually guide tomorrow," he answered and winked at Ernie motioning her to drink some water, which she did but then immediately let her head fall back into the comfort of the chair she was reclining in and closed her eyes.

"So, Hubbert outlines the change of human energy use from solar to coal, right?" Mac asked Laz rhetorically and continued quickly. "It was about the mid-1800s that oil and gas began to be exploited. It was also at this time that Britain found itself in the Industrial Revolution, a revolution brought about by the exploitation of concentrated solar energy formed millions of years ago: coal, oil, and gas. Hubbert then begins looking at the global rates of production for oil over time.

"He finds that between 1860 and 1930 the annual production doubled about every seven years, which is a nine percent annual increase. He combines this data with the observation that human population has been increasing at an unprecedented rate, especially during the first half of the twentieth century, and concludes that our population increase is due to the increasing exploitation of concentrated energy sources: coal, oil, and gas."

Mac stopped and took a long swig of water, looking up at the full moon again. As he began to shift his gaze back down towards his fellow campers he thought he saw something glide by the moon. As he looked back up he caught the tail end of the object as it passed beyond the moon, returning to a blackened background and disappear from sight. "I know bats don't tend to glide," he began. "Um, anything else fly at night out this way, Ernie?"

"Not that I'm aware of," she replied, opening her eyes slightly.

"Hmmm, that was weird. I thought I saw something about the size of a large bat or bird glide by the moon. Oh well, maybe I have a floater," Mac said shaking his head a little and sipping some more water.

"A floater?" Laz asked.

"Chances are you two are spared, for now," Mac answered. "As one gets older, the liquid in the eye accumulates debris. It's not a health concern, it's just that every once in a while they catch some light and cause a shadow on the retina, giving the sensation of a blurry image in your field of vision. I could have sworn, though, that I saw something.

"Anyways, Hubbert's shown how population increase has been brought about by increased access to concentrated energy, right? He then begins to argue that this is way out of the norm because for the previous tens of thousands of years the population was kept in check by the limited energy available from the sun.

"Based on rough estimates, he suggests humans probably doubled their population every thirty- to thirty-five thousand years until the recent past. What we've experienced recently is extremely abnormal and he estimates that the population has increased from about half a billion to over two billion in the last three hundred years; most of that growth occurring during the first half of the twentieth century, from 1900 to 1950."

Laz zoomed in on Mac, but not so close that he lost the bouncing of the shadows behind him. As he was watching the image on the camera's small LCD monitor, he thought he saw a faint shadow cross the scene. When he looked up into the sky he saw nothing but the moon and stars.

"But as we've already agreed the planet has finite resources, such as fossil fuels and minerals. So Hubbert concludes that the expansion humans have experienced must have physical limitations. Since the fossil fuels we've become dependent upon are useless once burned, we are using up a fixed store of concentrated energy that will eventually run out," Mac stressed and took another long drink from his canteen.

"So we'll run out of gas and oil some time down the road. We all know that but that's a long way off, isn't it?" Laz asked.

"Is it? Well, let me finish the tale and we can talk about that," Mac answered. "So here we are once again with a fixed stock of resources that we know will be depleted some day. Hubbert predicted over sixty years ago that global oil production would peak sometime in the late-1990s. Now, he was wrong about that; most people now agree that it occurred in 2005, but still he was right on with respect to the final endgame!" Mac declared with an enthusiastic flourish.

"If we look at Hubbert's curve again we know what happens after peak production." He took his stick and followed the curve back down with so much emphasis that the stick broke and he lost his balance, falling forward onto the ground.

"You okay?" Laz asked chuckling a bit, but making sure he had it all digitally-recorded, as Mac picked himself up and dusted off his clothes.

Ernie opened her eyes and lifted her head slightly. She was starting to feel a bit better and drank some more water.

"Yes, just my pride is hurt," Mac replied and sat back down. "Sorry folks, this stuff really gets me going. Now, back to my scary fireside tale," he began as he leaned forward and warmed himself a bit by the dying embers. "You know what, I'm going to be more careful this time." He picked up the larger part of the broken stick he had been using and got out of his chair, kneeling close to his first graph.

"Now, let's look at this idea of Hubbert's from a longer, historical perspective," he said as he drew a horizontal line about a metre long in the dirt. "Imagine this line represents about ten thousand years time, five thousand years before the present and five thousand years after, with us about here," he finished, placing a small line perpendicular to and bisecting the previous line about half-way along.

"Now, I'm going to show you how our fossil fuel energy sources would look from this time perspective," and he drew a relatively small and narrow Hubbert Curve just to the left of the centre. The curve went horizontally just above the zero line to both the right and left. "Here we sit today," he said as he placed an X on the down-slope of the curve, a bit beyond the peak.

"Holy shit," said Laz, as he leaned forward to record a close-up of Mac's drawings in the dirt.

"Exactly," Mac responded folding his legs and sitting down beside Ernie's chair, close to the fire.

"What about nuclear power? And solar and wind energy?" Ernie offered as she opened her eyes but still kept her head down.

"We can talk about alternatives later but suffice it to say that there is **no** other energy source available to us today or in the works that can replace the energy we are going to lose when fossil fuels run out. There is nothing comparable! Remember, we are only looking at having had access and use of this non-renewable, concentrated energy for a couple of centuries. Once it is gone, there are no second chances," Mac stated, frowning somewhat.

"Oh my," Ernie said as she rolled on her side slightly, bringing her legs up to her stomach in order to curl up a bit to fight the cold.

"Um-hmm," Laz agreed, as he stuffed another sushi into his mouth. "Hey, is that the highway we can hear?" he enquired between swallows.

Ernie tilted her head slightly, catching the faint buzz in the distance. "Yeah, I guess so. I can't recall hearing it ever before."

"Must be some big trucks out tonight, oh well, carry on Mac," Laz insisted, as he reached for yet another bit of sushi.

"Okay. So, Hubbert admits that during this relatively small time-frame humans have witnessed the most extraordinary of influences by the release of these discovered energy reserves. The problem, he argues, is that the transition back to the previous levels of energy and slow rates of change that characterised the previous five thousand or more years, and will characterise the next five thousand, will be extremely difficult to make because we've become used to and dependent upon exponential growth, and I love the concluding couple of sentences of his paper so much I've committed them to heart. Hubbert wrote that:

"'During the last two centuries we have known nothing but exponential growth and in parallel we have evolved what amounts to an exponential-growth culture, a culture so heavily dependent upon the continuance of exponential growth for its stability that it is incapable of reckoning with problems of non-growth. Since the problems confounding us are not intrinsically insoluble, it behooves us, while there is yet time, to begin a serious examination of the nature of our cultural constraints and of the cultural adjustments necessary to permit us to deal effectively with the problems rapidly arising.'

"In other words, we're fucked because this was written over sixty years ago and we've run out of time," Mac finished.

"Come on, it can't be as bad as you're making it out to be," Ernie said as she played with some of his hair that was hanging by her hand.

"Yeah maybe, but it sure is interesting, huh? I've spent some time during the past few years reading up on this stuff and-"

Suddenly, their evening went sideways.

The sound in the distance that they had attributed to the highway quickly became louder. Before they knew what was happening there was an explosion of rock, sand, metal, and flame only a few metres away. Mac, sitting by the fire, was blown off balance and landed face down where Ernie's chair had been only moments before. Ernie and Laz were blown backwards out of their chairs.

The force sent Ernie into a backwards shoulder roll. Apart from a few scrapes on her wrists and hands, she was fine. She got to her knees, relatively quickly. "What the," Ernie began and then screamed, "Laz!" She got up and ran towards her cousin who was lying on his back, not moving. He had been thrown back harder than Ernie as he was leaning forward, towards the blast.

Mac was quickly on his feet and came over. He knelt down to check on Laz. Placing one hand lightly on his chest, he reached for a wrist with the other and felt for a pulse. "He's still alive," he reassured Ernie. "There's a first aid kit in the trunk of Laz's car, on the left side, right against the trunk wall. Grab it," he directed Ernie, quickly removing his sweater and then taking off his t-shirt, placing it gently around a piece of metal sticking out of Laz's leg.

While Ernie retrieved the first aid kit, Mac checked Laz's head. There was a small lump forming behind his left ear, but no blood.

Ernie came back with the first aid kit. "Aren't you going to pull that thing out?" she asked.

"No," Mac responded. "I have no idea how deep it's gone or what it's cut into. I can stitch together skin but not muscle or blood vessels. It's best to stop the bleeding as much as possible; then I need to strap the metal in place so as to keep it from moving around. It's probably a good thing he's unconscious. First things first, take all the compress bandages and roll of tape out of the kit and just lay them there," Mac directed, nodding to a spot beside him.

"There's an instant ice pack in there as well. Get it cold and then hold it against the lump on the back of Laz's head. You'll find a bump coming up just behind his left ear," Mac instructed.

As Ernie busied herself with that task, Mac removed his shirt from Laz's leg. It wasn't bleeding a lot, which was positive, but the blood flow was steady. After cleaning the area with antiseptic wipes he applied a few compress bandages and used the roll of tape to secure them in place. He made sure the pressure was adequate then checked on Ernie.

"His leg's all bandaged up, how are you doing?" Mac asked, as he placed a hand on her shoulder.

"I'm okay. How's his leg?" Ernie enquired. It was obvious by the pitch and tone that stress was beginning to affect her.

"It's fine. The bleeding has almost stopped. Here, let me take that," he replied as he eased her hand away from the ice pack, noticing that she was shaking slightly.

"What the hell was that thing?" she began to sound frantic.

He knew he needed to give her something to do, away from Laz and this area. He laid the ice pack on the ground and rested Laz's head on it.

"Listen, you need to pack everything in the cabin. I know I haven't moved anything in yet but I'm not sure about Laz. Go pack whatever you find. We need to get Laz some medical attention." Mac had gently led Ernie away from the scene and to the front of the cabin. He opened the door and steered her inside, leaving her to pack.

He walked over towards the impact point in the coulee wall. There were shards of metal, plastic, glass and what appeared to be a plane's wing, but a small one, obviously. The entire plane couldn't have been much more than two metres in length.

As he got closer he noticed markings on the wing. Mac immediately recognised what it was. It was a Canadian military symbol; this was a military drone.

He ran back to the campfire. "Ernie, we have to get out of here," he yelled towards the cabin. She was just coming out. "We need to get Laz into his car. Throw everything in your car then meet me back here. We're going to have the military here in short order," Mac explained as he went to grab the video camera that had landed not far from Laz in a patch of dry brush. It was still recording so he quickly got footage of the entire scene and close-ups of the wing that indicated it was a Canadian military vehicle. When the hell did the Canadian military start using unmanned drones domestically, he asked himself.

Against the grain should be a way of life
What's worth the prize is always worth the fight
Every second counts 'cause there's no second try
So live like you'll never live it twice
Don't take the free ride in your own life
If today was your last day
And tomorrow was too late
Could you say goodbye to yesterday?
Would you live each moment like your last?

Nickelback, 2008
If Today Was Your Last Day, Dark Horse

April 3, 7:00 am

Sam took a deep breath and looked up from his pizza. Sparkling, light green eyes peered back at him. "I can't do it MA. As much as it would be the easiest thing to agree to, I can't do it. The timing is just not good at all," he finished, fighting the tears he could feel forming in his eyes.

Maria-Antonia Vasconcelos, a fellow third-year student, gripped Sam's hand a little harder. Sam and MA had been together for a few months now. Sam had to admit that the speed of their romance had caught them both by surprise. Neither had been looking. Well, that was not entirely true, Sam was looking all the time but never finding the courage to act. MA had to make the first move.

At least that was the way Sam remembered it. He had simply forgotten his glasses one class. Although he'd be able to read his textbook and notes, he would not be able to see anything the professor placed on the board at the front of the lecture room they were in. He'd seen an attractive girl a few seats away and simply asked if he could copy her notes, he'd forgotten his glasses.

They had chatted during the break and he found out that she was a first generation Canadian of Brazilian parents. She had just returned from Brazil, spending the summer helping to build an elementary school. She was returning after the academic year to help complete the building and stock the school with resources.

At the end of the class, Sam offered to buy her a coffee or tea for the use of her notes. She accepted and they headed towards the nearest campus café. After a lovely half-hour of listening to her thoughts on the evolution of intelligence, Sam thanked her once again and headed off to his next class.

That was the fall that Sam's dad had his first heart attack. Sam ended up dropping all but one course that term. He spent his time helping his mother get his father back on his feet. To be honest, Sam had rarely thought of MA after that class. He was worried about his father.

MA, however, remembered their first encounter very differently. She had seen an attractive classmate approach her, ask for help, reimburse her for the help, listen attentively to her talk for the entire time, and ask for nothing in return. She knew he wanted to ask her out and he would, he just hadn't realised it yet.

When he didn't return after that last class, where he'd 'forgotten his glasses', MA grew concerned. In speaking to Sam, she learned that he was a committed student and that learning was his passion. He loved the constant challenge of learning something new so he was taking the course on statistics in order to learn more about probability as it related to scientific conclusions. He believed that science was just a model of how the world worked, it could never tell us what reality was truly like. Probability was just a way of not really having to say, 'I'm pretty sure, but not entirely.'

She had also learned his name, that he lived in town with his parents and siblings, and most importantly that he was not dating anyone. She mailed him a Season's Greeting card during the winter break with a note that she had enjoyed their 'date' and hoped all was well, not seeing him in class anymore. She asked him to give her a call some time and included her phone number. Sam had called and asked her out minutes after reading the card.

Their first official date was shortly after the second term began. Sam's dad had bounced back relatively quickly from his heart attack and Sam had returned to school full-time. In less than a month, Sam was sleeping at MA's fairly regularly. After three months, Sam had proposed.

"And I can't do what you're asking. Maybe it's not meant to be, not right now," she replied. Those last few words hung in the air between them, hovering over the ring that still lay on the table. The music suddenly got louder and began to irritate Sam's ears. He closed his eyes and fought the tears that began rolling down his cheeks. He didn't want to lose MA, not again. The music got increasingly louder.

…Sam bolted upright from his sleep. Christ, he hated that dream. His heart was pounding and he had been sweating so much his bed-sheets were soaked. He put his head in his hands and found that his cheeks were wet. He had been crying.

He reached out and knocked over his manual alarm clock as he turned it off. It hit the floor with a clang and then started ringing again. Sam reached over and turned it off, then let his head flop back down onto his pillow for a moment to gather his thoughts.

Sam and MA had spent the last part of that term constantly in each other's company, knowing that she was returning to Brazil for the next twelve to fourteen months at the end of exams. They had promised to stay in touch and pick up the conversation about marriage after MA returned. In the meantime, Sam would try to book a flight to visit during the winter break.

Tragically, the small plane MA had taken from Cuiaba to a smaller airport close to the Bolivian-Brazilian border had gone down in the rainforest. The area was too dense and remote for much more than helicopter surveillance. Based on the wreckage pattern, the Brazilian military reported that no survivors were expected.

Sam knew he had never fully recovered from that loss as he really thought they were meant to be together. Sam rarely made romantic connections, feeling lost whenever he was around women. Losing MA had been almost as devastating as losing his mother, maybe more so. He had not been in a serious relationship since.

He could see that the sun was coming up so he shook off the remnants of the dream, sat up and got out of bed to begin his morning exercise routine. Focus he told himself, this was no time to be getting emotional. He'd had the profound pleasure of a lovely woman's company for five months, more than if he'd never met her. It was better than having not known her at all.

Sam was heading north today and needed to make sure everything was ready. After a quick bite to eat and some personal chores, he reviewed for the last time the items that would go into his knapsack. He checked off his list of items as he placed them in his knapsack, making sure the items he would need frequently and sooner were on top of supplies that he would not need for at least a few days.

Whether water or shelter was of primary concern depended entirely upon the situation. He had water purification tablets, a personal water filtration system, and carried two litres of water in his canteen. He was not going to be exerting his body enough to lose too much water through his sweat. He knew, however, that two litres would not get him very far if there were no other sources of water. Even without all the dehydrated food he would be consuming, he would still lose enough water through his urine and constant breathing to need to consume water regularly. As he would be traveling at a time of year when snow could still be found and the many rivers he would be passing would be at or near their spring highs, water was not a concern. He set the canteen aside as he would be carrying it independent of his knapsack, but his purifying tablets and filter he placed in a pouch on the outside of his knapsack for easy access.

As he packed his items, he reflected on the unusual amount of snow this past winter. The amount of snow his area had received the past few months was abnormally high. The trend for the past few years had been less snow but more extreme temperature changes. In fact, the temperature had been so abnormal that one of his favourite aperitifs, ice-wine from the Niagara region, had not been produced for two years in a row now. The lack of snow had put a tremendous stress on what little agricultural land was left in Ontario.

Thinking about the lack of agricultural land caused Sam to recall one of the stories his father had shared with him when he was young. His father had grown up thinking that all the farmland surrounding the small town he was born and grew up in would last forever. It was Sam's first lesson on exponential growth...

"It's a really simple mathematical concept, Sam," Joel Gregory told his eldest son. "The rate of increase—or percentage of growth—can speed or slow the process. Suppose a town increases in size five percent per year. At that rate, it will double in size after fourteen years and double again in another fourteen years. So a city starting at twenty thousand people will, at five percent growth per year, reach eighty thousand after twenty-eight years. For the average person—who lives about eighty years—what size will that town of twenty thousand at the time of their birth reach at the end of his or her life?"

"I hate when you give me math questions and no paper, Dad," Sam said, slouching slightly.

"That's what a brain is for. You can't always depend on your technological gadgets. Like a pencil or paper," his father teased him, smiling.

"You're such a Luddite, Dad," Sam quipped in return.

"How many?" his fathered repeated, pointing to his own head reminding Sam to use his brain.

"Okay, let's look at the pattern based on the doubling time of fourteen years. Twenty thousand at zero—forty thousand after fourteen years—eighty thousand after twenty-eight years—one hundred and sixty thousand after forty-two years—three hundred and twenty thousand after fifty-six years—six hundred and forty thousand after seventy years—and," he paused for a moment. "About a million after eighty years. I'd need a calculator to figure out the exact number. So after an average person's life the town of twenty thousand had grown to about one million. Holy shit, Dad!" Sam responded, shocked at how quickly the number grew.

"Language, Sam," his father reminded him sternly.

"Holy Shit!" said Dave smiling, who was sitting right beside Sam in his high chair.

"You're explaining that to your mother, Sam," stated their father, looking directly at Sam and trying very hard to suppress a smile. "Anyways, that is exactly what had happened to my hometown. Thinking like every other town's council, the ones in my hometown believed growth was the way for their town to prosper so they pushed for growth to occur as quickly as possible. There was no agricultural land remaining by the time I moved away. Yes, some had prospered, especially those who benefited from growth, like the development industry, the banks, oh, and of course, the local government. But the council never considered the negative aspects of such growth as well: perpetually increasing taxes and government bureaucracy, and increased pollution, poverty, and crime, just to name a few. I moved out the first chance I got."

"Holy shit, Sam!" said his brother again, only adding his name this time.

...Sam couldn't help but smile at the memory of his three-year old brother repeating that phrase for the first time in front of his mother. It was a priceless moment of shock and disbelief that was frozen into his memory as if it had just happened. He laughed to himself and continued down his checklist.

For his shelter needs he had a lightweight, two-person tent and a synthetic-fibre, sleeping bag rated for sub-zero temperatures. He would have preferred a lighter and less bulky down sleeping bag but an early canoe trip with his family had ended his relationship with down. He had dropped his down sleeping bag getting out of the canoe one late afternoon. It never dried fully and he did not enjoy the rest of the trip.

In case he needed to fashion his own shelter, he had a parang, folding hunting knife, folding shovel, flexible saw, and twenty metres of polyethylene rope. He could build a number of shelters with this gear. If worse came to worse, he could crawl inside the large plastic bag he had. It would be wet, but he'd stay more than warm enough for this time of year.

He picked up the parang, observing that the blade needed some attention. There were a few nicks that hadn't been ground out yet. He loved this Indonesian-style blade he had purchased a few years ago. It was much better at hacking through underbrush than the machete he had used in the past. The parang's sweet spot was further forward than that on a machete, so the heavier parang blade would cut through forest underbrush with no second thought, while protecting the bearer's knuckles as a bonus. The parang also hosted three different cutting edges in the single blade. The edge near the handle could be used for carving, the middle section was the chopping edge, and the further edge was the sharpest and could be used for skinning animals.

His mess kit consisted of a personal Swedish Svea stove and a litre of naphtha fuel for it; tea bags—although he preferred the taste of coffee, it didn't quench thirst like tea could; and enough food to get him through three weeks. Just in case, however, he also had some fishing line and hooks, and 2 metres of snare wire. His food supplies made up the largest portion of his pack's volume and weight.

Other gear included: a magnifying glass; flint; waterproofed matches; candles; a change of clothes; waterproof jacket and pants; an extra pair of shoes; a mirror; three flares; two thermal Mylar blankets; a compass and topographic map of the area; needles and thread; and, most importantly, a roll of toilet paper. Seeing that he still had a bit of room, he added a second roll of toilet paper, just in case.

Hi picked up the potassium iodide tablets and said out loud, "We couldn't be that stupid could we?" The tablets were precautionary;

they would help prevent thyroid cancer from radioactive potassium iodine nucleotides in case of a nuclear explosion.

Sam thought about the nuclear situation for a moment. The five nations with the most nuclear weapons—the U.S., Russia, France, the U.K., and China—had all signed the *Treaty on the Non-Proliferation of Nuclear Weapons* with most other countries in the world, but they still held almost twenty thousand nuclear warheads between them.

The U.S. had been the only country in the world to use such weapons against other humans so far, but it was not entirely unimaginable that a scenario could play out where a mistake, misinterpretation, or technological glitch lead to a strike of some kind.

While Sam was well aware of the impact energy resource depletion could have on society. He also knew that an empire with its back to the wall was capable of anything and a lot of what was transpiring across the world was political empire building, or collapse, he thought. Unfortunately, there was enough posturing going on in the Middle East between the nuclear powers to warrant concern. All because of oil and our desire for its relatively cheap, concentrated energy, Sam thought sadly.

One of the more potent changes to convince Sam that it was time to go north had been the government's response to the growing protest movement. As the government passed laws to give itself greater control and power, the movement grew in response. This was a race no one could win without someone getting hurt badly.

In its latest bill, the government created Canada's version of the *American Patriot Act. The Canadian Act to Prevent Terror and Terrorists* (*CAPT-T*) and accompanying legislation was contained in a sweeping omnibus budget bill that altered almost every previous act of Parliament. The first move was to nationalize all Internet service providers and then restrict Internet access to websites and URLs only approved by a new federal oversight committee.

Boy, things had deteriorated quickly after this was passed, Sam thought. First was Quebec. The 'Student Riot' of 2012 had been simmering in the background for some time. Support for the growing protest had spread throughout the province. In fact, the harder the provincial government tried to stamp out public dissent, the more widespread the dissent grew.

Seeing the protest movement gather steam, the majority federal government passed *CAPT-T* without even bringing it to parliament. While opposition parties attempted to make political hay of the situation, there was little to be done. For some time, the government had been testing the limits of its authority and circumventing parliament.

Precedents had been set. The prime minister declared that parliament was just slowing down its ability to deal with emergency situations. It passed the act and began to implement its laws.

One of the unintended consequences of this move, however, was that Occupier groups sprang up in every city or town with a university or college. It wasn't long after this that the Occupiers focused all their protests in just four cities outside Quebec: Ottawa, Toronto, Vancouver, and Calgary. Days later, the country instituted a national state of emergency.

Sam had made the decision to head north and see how the situation evolved. Most of Ontario's population had migrated to the cities of Ottawa or Toronto. He was fairly certain that more peripheral areas outside of the core would be far down on the list of priorities for the government and their emergency efforts. If things turned even more chaotic, he did not want to be too close to the Greater Toronto Area and its millions of people.

Sam knew that over the time it would take him to hike north, most of his gear would not be necessary. One of the things he had learned, however, was to build some redundancy, or insurance, into his personal systems. His homes were warmed by several means—natural gas, wood, and sunlight—so that should one fail or be temporarily unavailable, he had the others for backup.

His southern home was located in a community with several sources of food and water. Supplemented by his own gardening and water systems, he could survive independent of government support or infrastructure without too much effort. Self-sufficiency had been an increasing part of his life since his growing realisation that one could not depend on government or corporations to choose the right path to sustainability. Short-term profits always took precedent.

Sam was also aware that he could not predict the future any better than a meteorologist could predict the weather; the further out from the present, the more the range of possibilities and the more variables that came into play. In addition there were positive and negative feedback loops, some acting quickly and others with long delays; and then there were the black swans.

Sam placed the last of his gear into his pack and took a few deep breaths as he put the knapsack over his right shoulder. He had already made sure everything was secure and safe, so all that was left was to lock the front door. He turned around to look one more time at his home. He'd left three letters on the table by the front door, one for his sister, one for his brother, and one for his dad.

They were all copies of the same Word document that he had printed out some time ago, when he had made the decision to go north should things turn as bad as he thought they could. The last line or two of each, however, had been personalized. Early this morning, just after he'd eaten, he had added a couple of hand-written lines to each then sealed them. Channeling the last of his resolve he took a deep breath and shut the door, locking it behind him.

He decided that he would stick to lesser-traveled roads, not that he expected too many vehicles to be anywhere. There had been no gasoline available outside of certain urban centres for weeks. For a while people had been able to get what they needed through the black market that quickly developed as prices jumped and shortages grew. The one thing that the black market did was speed the flight from Canada's rural and suburban areas to its urban centres.

Sam adjusted the pack as he began his trek. It felt good on his back; of course it was still early in the day, not to mention early in this whole predicament he found himself in. He hadn't walked more than a couple hundred metres when a cat began to follow him. This is not what I need, he thought, but he didn't have the heart to scare it away. He stopped and let the cat catch up. It was a perfect example of a tuxedo cat; solid black except for some white on its paws, belly, and face.

It was obviously someone's pet as it strode right up to Sam and began curling around his leg, purring loudly. "And, what are we going to call you, pal?" Sam asked as he bent down on one knee to stroke the cat's back.

After a moment's thought, Sam came up with it. "Okay, Tux. How long since you've seen anyone?" Sam asked as he continued stroking the cat's back. He stopped his hand near the cat's belly to see how it was getting on. "You've been eating well, I see," he told the cat and brought his other hand in to help lift the back of the cat. "And, you're male. Glad to have another fellow along for the ride but you'll have to provide for yourself, buddy. I've not got much you'd like," he finished. Sam rose and continued walking. The cat leisurely followed.

"So, what's your story, Tux? Did your family take off and leave you? Or were you just unlucky and found yourself out hunting while things were falling apart here?" Sam looked down at the cat that followed about a half metre behind and to his left.

God I hate cats, Sam thought. Well, it wasn't that he hated them. He just didn't really find much use for them. Sure, they were cute as kittens but then they just slept, ate, and howled all night. At least that's what his sister's cat had done when they were growing up. She had named her cat Dumbledore after the famous Harry Potter series' professor. Sam, however, had taught Dave to call it Dummydork. This lesson served its purpose perfectly. It drove Susie mad.

Following the road he had decided to start on, Sam saw the only neighbour he knew of who had remained. It looked as though he was out working on his garden. As he drew closer Sam yelled, "Shane, you're out early to work on the yard."

"Hey, good morning Sam. Yeah, I thought I'd get a bit of the heavy work done before Caera's up. Today's the day is it?" Shane asked, hoping that perhaps Sam had changed his mind.

"Yep, heading out now. Look, if you really need anything-"

Shane interrupted him, "Sam, you have been more than generous in everything you've done for Caera and me ever since we moved here. You've been a saint. Thank you for your offer but we've got everything we need right here. With your garden on top of ours we'll have plenty of food for a small family," he replied, winking at Sam.

"Well, practice makes perfect, right?" Sam asked rhetorically in response. "You don't recognise this cat do you?" Sam asked pointing to the cat wrapped around his leg.

Shane looked down at the cat. "Nope. Look, I take it you haven't heard anything else about what's happening?"

"Nothing, sorry. As I've said before, I'm going to go north for a while. You may," Sam paused taking a deep breath. "You might see my brother or sister around sometime, please let them know I'm okay and I headed north today." He paused again for a moment, thinking of his brother and sister. "So, I'm off and hopefully our paths will cross again sometime in the future. If I get a sense or information that things have settled down, I'll probably come back down this way. All the best, Shane," Sam said, leaning forward and offering his hand.

"You too, Sam. Um," Shane paused not quite sure what to say. "Take care of yourself and I'm sure we will see each other again. You know where we are," he said thumbing towards his house. "And you're always welcome," Shane offered, as he withdrew his hand from the shake.

"Take care," Sam finished. Not wanting to prolong an uncomfortable moment, he turned and walked away. "Come on Tux, I've got some great cat jokes."

The sun was beginning to warm the air and Sam rolled his head from side-to-side, releasing some of the tension that had been building. It seemed to have grown since he decided it was time to head north. Tux ran ahead on the road for a ways, stopping by a driveway mailbox. He lay down at the end of the driveway and stretched out, waiting for Sam to catch up it appeared.

He'd been walking for about two hours or more, chatting with Tux on and off, when he began thinking about black swans. How many people, he thought, expected everything to fall apart so quickly? Probably not too damn many.

Throughout the ages there were prognostications about global collapse. Books had been written and documentaries had been made. But if humans had a fatal flaw, Sam thought, it was not being able to think about the long-term consequences of their actions in a serious and thoughtful manner. Humans seemed to be wired to focus on short-term goals only, even when it was obvious that to reach the short-term goals, the long-term health of humans and/or the planet would be compromised. It was as if it was impossible for collective delay of gratification.

His thinking faltered as he tried to focus on avoiding the cat that had now decided to walk in between his feet. Quite unexpectedly, he thought he heard someone crying. As he approached a corner property, he could distinctly hear a woman sobbing.

He turned the corner and oriented to the sound. He saw her then, a very attractive East Indian woman sitting on the porch of a beautiful country home. A Bed & Breakfast sign was swinging gently in the breeze by the road.

The woman had her head in her hands and was crying quite steadily. Sam approached tentatively, calling out so as to not startle her. "Hello."

She looked up and reacted with a look of disbelief. Wiping at her eyes with the dishcloth she was carrying in her hand, she placed her other hand on the column beside her and stood, unnoticed by Sam, somewhat awkwardly.

"Hello," she replied, smiling slightly. She continued to wipe at some lingering tears.

"I'm sorry if I startled you. My name is Sam, Sam Gregory." He reached up from the bottom of the stairs, offering his hand.

She backed up a step and put up her hands. "My, ah," she paused wiping at her eyes again. "My husband is really sick and I don't know if I'm contagious."

"How long has he been sick?" Sam asked, his mind quickly accessing his first aid training.

"Probably four months," she replied then began sobbing again.

"If it's been four months and you haven't shown any signs. I think you're safe. What are your husband's symptoms, if you don't mind me asking?" he probed as he came up the steps.

"Are you a doctor?" the woman asked, obviously hopeful.

"No, but I have some advanced first aid training so I might be able to help. If I can't, I know someone who can," Sam responded calmly, knowing that this woman was clearly in a stressful situation and needed a calm environment to be able to think properly and help him.

"Well, the weekend of the Toronto Occupier Riot in early December last year he began showing," she stopped and looked down for a moment. "I'm sorry, my name is Chandra Saini. You introduced yourself and I didn't, I'm sorry," she replied looking up into his eyes.

"Not a problem whatsoever, you have a sick husband and your thoughts should be about him, I understand. So what are the symptoms Chandra?" Sam asked again, being ever more alert to this woman's emotional state, not wanting to upset her.

"Well, he had been doing some strenuous activity the night before the riot because we had lost power in our building. He was up and down the stairs a few times, but that shouldn't be a concern because he was in great shape, he exercised all the time," Chandra shared as she indicated for him to sit in one of the wicker chairs on the front porch.

"Okay, well whatever you can remember would be great. Major symptoms would be particularly helpful," Sam clarified, sitting after removing his knapsack.

"Well the biggest issue I think has been the intestinal distress, severe pain and diarrhea. He's had the intestinal problems pretty well the whole time we've been away. He's had no energy, I can't get him to eat much, and he's lost so much weight. I don't know what to do," Chandra informed him, her voice still filled with distress.

Sam sighed inwardly as he knew this was beyond his basic survival medicine. He would have to get this man back to Caera. "Okay, this is beyond my first aid skills but I happen to know where there is a very experienced nurse not too far from here. Is your husband able to travel, do you have a car?"

"Um, he can walk a little. But he's just so-" she trailed off as tears began to fill her eyes again.

"It's okay. Listen to me Chandra," Sam said as he took her hands in his. "Can I meet your husband? What's his name?"

"Ranj—Ranjeet," Chandra said as she sniffled, responding to his gentle, calming touch.

"Okay, we need to get Ranjeet to a friend of mine. She's a nurse and will know a lot more than me. Can I meet Ranjeet?" Sam asked, gently helping her up from her chair.

"Sure, he's just inside on the couch," she said then turned to lead him inside. "Ranj honey, we have a visitor."

"A visitor?" responded a gravelly voice.

Sam followed Chandra in. Sitting on the couch was an obviously sick young man. He appeared to have lost a lot of weight; his skin seemed to hang on him.

"Sorry if I don't get up," Ranjeet said, "I haven't been feeling the best lately."

"Yes, your wife was telling me. Ranjeet, my name is Sam Gregory. If you think you're up to it, I know a nurse who is still nearby. It's about twenty kilometres but if you have a car we c-"

"No car, I'm sorry I didn't get that far," Chandra interrupted. "We traded our car to be able to stay here. We're actually supposed to be moving into the house under construction next door. Today," she added but then couldn't hold back the tears any longer. She dropped down beside her husband, burying her head in his shoulder, sobbing.

Not being able to raise his arms, Ranjeet just patted his wife's leg. "It's okay, baby. Everything's gonna be okay."

Sadly, we believe the world will experience overshoot and collapse in global resource use and emissions much the same way as the dot.com bubble--though on a much longer time scale. The growth phase will be welcomed and celebrated, even long after it has moved into unsustainable territory (this we know, because it has already happened). The collapse will arrive very suddenly, much to everyone's surprise. And once it has lasted for some years, it will become increasingly obvious that the situation before the collapse was totally unsustainable. After more years of decline, few will believe it will ever end. Few will believe that there once more will be abundant energy and sufficient wild fish.

Dennis Meadows et al., 2004
Limits to Growth: The 30-Year Update

April 3, 8:00 a.m.

Dave began to slow down when he heard the child yelling, "Daddy!" And it appeared to Dave that once the child saw that he was not her father, she began to hesitate as well. The other adult, however, did not break stride. She overtook the child just as everyone came to a stop.

"Who are you?" she stated firmly, standing between the child and Dave.

"Hi, I'm sor-, I'm sorry," Dave sputtered a little embarrassed. "I'm Dave. I thought the child here was in danger," he said trying to make eye contact with her as she looked around from behind the older girl. "I'm assuming I was wrong," he finished between deep breaths caused by the quick sprint he'd just run while wearing a fully-laden knapsack. He raised his hands slightly, palms towards the two girls and backed up a step.

"No, I'm not in danger, I'm Kat and this is my sister Marissa," Kat stated without any outward sign of fear, stepping out from behind her sister. "Do you know what happened to our parents?"

"Your parents?" Dave asked back in return, somewhat shocked by her question.

"They left for the Occupier protest in Toronto early last December," Kat replied, as Marissa grabbed her by the arm and pulled back towards her, making sure she was out of this man's reach. "The last we heard was that the government had announced a state of emergency. The radios went dead and we lost power not long after that," Kat finished as Marissa began backing them up a bit.

"Well," Dave paused, giving himself a moment to think. "If you had radios, you know as much as me. There's been no news getting out to anyone as far as I know. I've been walking for the past three days from my place to the west. I'm going to my brother's, just a day or so east of here."

He finally looked up from the younger girl and looked at the older one. He swore he knew her from somewhere, she looked strikingly familiar.

"So," he began, not being able to tear his gaze away from her, "um—you two—alone?" He seemed to be having trouble getting his words out.

"Yes. We've been alone," Marissa replied as she too felt like she recognised this young man. Maybe he was a student at the university, she thought. She began to smile, returning his gaze, "Do you-"

Kat cut off Marissa's question. "Are you going to kill us?" Kat asked in perfect seriousness.

"Katsumi!" her sister said in rebuke.

"I need to know if he's going to kill us or not. If he's not, then I'm having breakfast because I'm hungry and need to get on with my day," she said as she began to turn. "It's Dave, right?"

Dave just nodded, still feeling a bit off by the presence of this woman standing near him.

"Dave, are you going to kill us?" Kat asked him again.

"No kill," Dave muttered feeling like his tongue had turned into sodden wool.

"Have you eaten?" Kat prodded.

"No eat," Dave responded, his mind completely occupied in an attempt to figure out how he knew this girl. Something was wrong; he couldn't multitask at the moment.

"I'm making some tea and warming some porridge," Kat yelled over her shoulder as she walked away, returning to her home.

Not five minutes later they were all huddled around the kitchen table. Kat did most of the talking as Dave and Marissa continued to sneak glances at each other. She tried to fill Dave in on their past four months with just a few succinct points: they had been burning wood to keep warm; had enough food and supplies to get them through the winter; and, had cooked using their BBQ and an old Coleman stove.

Dave was beginning to feel some clarity returning. He had begun to string full sentences together. "How are your supplies holding out?" he asked at the end of her summary, looking at Marissa.

"To be honest we're getting low," Kat began. "We haven't really talked about what we're going to do."

Dave noticed that Marissa's hands were shaking as her sister spoke. "Are you okay?" he asked as gently as possible.

"Yeah, I just," she began, and then paused to take a deep breath and exhale once. "I just get anxious sometimes and we've been so worried about our parents, and I don't know what I'm going to do about our food and I-"

"It's okay," Dave said as he placed his hand on top of one of her shaking hands.

Marissa looked down and only after a few seconds pause did she pull her hand away, somewhat abruptly.

"Oh, I'm sorry, I didn't mean anything," Dave responded quickly.

"No. It's just that that's what my mum would do when I got nervous. That's all," Marissa said. She felt something quite odd at his touch and it left her unsettled.

"Got it," Dave responded, not wanting to begin speaking mumbo jumbo again but his brain was still not fully functional. "Come with me," he blurted out.

"Yeah, let's go," Kat said quickly, wanting the excitement of a trip away from their home.

"Listen, I know it sounds strange as we just met, but you are welcome to join me. You could come to my brother's. He's got everything we need and you'll be safer with more people," Dave said, making his case but trying not to sound as if he were pleading.

"Hang on just a minute, Kat. We don't know if Mum and Dad are on their way here right now or not. We can't just run off from home with someone we've just met," Marissa explained to her little sister.

Kat stood and began to walk away from the kitchen table, "Marissa, they've been gone for four months. They're not coming back and we're low on supplies." With that, Kat walked out of the kitchen and yelled back towards Marissa, "I'm getting packed."

Dave just pursed his lip a bit and looked away a bit embarrassed. "Um, I'm sorry. I didn't mean to start a family feud."

"No, she's right," Marissa admitted and looked down feeling more lost than ever. She had been avoiding the nagging reality about her parents for as long as she could. "I've been thinking the same thing. I just can't-" she trailed off, fighting to calm her breathing.

"Well, before you actually make a decision let me show you where we are and where I was heading. It's only about a day's walk, maybe a little more for Kat's shorter legs," Dave offered. Marissa smiled at his attempted humour.

She didn't know if she could trust this man. He had just shown up out of the blue and then offered to have them accompany him. Even though she had the feeling that she knew him—her mind was racing.

Dave got the map from his knapsack and spread it out on the kitchen table. He indicated about where he thought they were on the map and where he was heading. He was beginning to feel more at ease, like he would with a close friend. "Depending on how Kat makes out, we might get there by midday tomorrow. Maybe even later today," he added optimistically.

"Don't worry about Kat. We'd both have trouble keeping up with her," Marissa smiled. She was beginning to feel more comfortable with this young man, whom she couldn't help but notice had a very athletic build.

"Listen," Dave began, keeping his voice down so Kat wouldn't hear, "I do have a little bit more information about Toronto. But I'm not sure if your sister should hear it or not."

"Hear what?" asked Kat, returning to the kitchen from a different door, surprising Dave.

"Oh, I," he stopped, looking at Marissa for some guidance.

"She's a lot hardier than me Dave. You can tell us, it's okay," Marissa urged, knowing her sister would pester them endlessly if she wasn't told.

Taking a deep breath, Dave sat down. He still wouldn't share everything, but he could share enough to put these girls at some ease.

"Just before I left I had a neighbour make it home from Toronto. He'd been there when the riot began and it took him almost four months to get home. He said he was lucky to get out without getting caught up in what he called a prison camp."

"Prison camp?" Marissa stuttered.

"Have you ever seen the classic movie with Kurt Russell called *Escape from New York*?" Dave asked them. They both shook their heads. "Probably a good thing," Dave continued, as he'd thought about the analogy a bit more. "It's not a perfect example anyways. Um, what do you know? Just what happened before the radio stations went off the air, right?" Marissa and Kat both nodded. "And you heard the announcement about the state of emergency?" Dave continued. They nodded again.

"Okay, Jim, a neighbour of mine, was at his brother's in Toronto to go to a Leaf's game when the riot began. He got stuck at his brother's place close to Queen's Park. They were pretty high up and had a good view of what was going on most of the time. First, let me say that Jim said that once the third day passed, there were regular food deliveries to local markets by the government. So long as people remained indoors and followed the government's rules around when they could be outside, no one else was being arrested. And, he said that while there were a lot of injuries, there were no reports of casualties. Anyways, to try and make a long story a bit shorter, they watched as the police and military closed in on all sides of the protesters for the first few days. They were all-" he searched for the word.

"Corralled like cattle," Marissa offered, her hands starting to shake slightly again, but from anger not anxiety.

"Yeah, I guess that would be a good description. They were corralled into the core close to Queen's Park, and they weren't allowed to leave. In fact, waves of security forced more and more people into that area, and they didn't appear to be letting anyone in or out, as far as Jim knew."

"Not letting anyone in or out?" Kat asked, looking at his sister with some concern. But concern for her sister's reaction, not for her parents.

"Jim said a lot of people fleeing the area were telling him that. He said that security was rounding up anyone on the street and forcibly taking them into holding cells all around the Queen's Park area. Now remember," Dave said trying to keep things calm, "there have been no reports of casualties so, if your parents were in the area and with relatives, I'm sure they're okay."

"Yes, yes," Marissa said, trying to reassure herself. "My Aunt lives right near Queen's Park as well and they were staying there." She could feel her heart begin to pound harder in her chest and took some deep breaths to try and calm her body as it reacted to the building stress.

"Well, I'm sure they're all there," Dave responded as he looked down at his hands. Marissa had taken hold of them and was gripping them tightly. "Um," he began, as he slipped the bottom hand out and covered hers with it. "Ah," he tried to continue. He was at a total loss for words for only the second time in his life that he could remember. The first was not 30 minutes ago when he first looked into those hazel eyes he was now lost in. He glanced over at Kat who was just smiling at him with a silly grin that read 'cat got your tongue pal?'

"So chances are that they are stuck in the centre of Toronto," Kat began. "With the security perimeter and loss of power they may never get home, but chances are also good that they are fine and with Aunt Kimiko. Oh and Mar," she said looking at her sister and pointing to the pair of hands now entwined on the table.

Marissa went totally red, she couldn't help it. "I'm so sorry," she said, looking away from Dave. "I-I don't know what I was thinking," she stammered but did not withdraw her hands nearly as quickly as the last time, letting them linger a bit.

"No-no problem," Dave stammered back. He was just as embarrassed, but he was feeling something else as well. Marissa's hands had just felt 'natural' in his, like they'd always been there. He wanted to hold them again.

He laid his cards on the table. "Look, I'm heading east to my brother Sam's. He's been preparing for something like this for a long time and you're welcome to join me. There would be at least four of us then. You two need to decide between you, though. I can't make any promises about your parents. It has been four months."

Kat and Marissa looked at each other. "What do you think, Mar? Do we have enough food to keep us going? Tell me we'll be okay and I'll wait here with you for Mum and Dad." Kat moved from her chair and went to her older sister. She crawled up into her lap like she used to as a toddler and put her arms around her older sister. Marissa couldn't help herself, she began to cry. Then Kat started to cry.

Dave thought, 'girls, can't live with them. Ah, pass the beer nuts'; a great line from an old television show that his dad had on DVD, *Cheers*. Regardless, he had to reassure these two girls and validate their concern for their absent parents.

"Have you got a place that only your parents would look?" he began as calmly as possible. "Somewhere we could leave directions to my brother's. It's maybe a day, day and a half east of here; not very far at all. I can leave a detailed map if we know it will be safe. I don't want to leave maps to my brother's house all over the province," he finished, while sweeping his hand about trying to lighten the mood a bit.

Marissa wiped at her sister's tears and kissed her on the cheek. "Yes, there is a place in their bedroom that I can leave a note. My mum knows to look behind her bathroom mirror for a note if we're not around. We used to do that in our old house," she answered as Kat began to wipe at her sister's tears. "I know our food won't last much longer and I don't know if we could grow enough to survive. Why did they never teach us some of these basic skills in school?"

"Good question, but for another day," Kat exclaimed. She jumped out of her sister's lap and looked at Dave, "When do we leave?"

"It's about a day's walk from here. We'll need some food and water before we head out. It needs to be at least enough for you two for the day and then a bit extra just in case. Let's put a few things together and then we can leave. If we don't have any problems on the way, we could even make it before dark," Dave answered having semi-regained his composure once again, at least for the moment.

"Well, Mar?" Kat looked at her sister with raised eyebrows.

"You go see if you can find our two knapsacks in the basement, Kat. I'll see what's in the kitchen," Marissa replied hesitantly. She still wasn't sure about any of this. Just a few short months ago she was completing her term at school, more worried about the exams and papers she had to write than anything else.

In less than ten seconds Kat had returned with the two knapsacks. "I had them in the other room," she announced proudly, grinning from ear-to-ear.

"Okay," Marissa replied, pausing to give herself a moment to think. "You take Dave to show him what supplies we have left in the root cellar. Just in case there's anything there you think we should take," Marissa added, looking at Dave. "I need to write a letter and pack a few things."

Within 30 minutes they were ready to go. Dave had made sure they packed appropriately. There wasn't a lot to take as Sam would have plenty. And besides, Dave thought, it's only a day's walk back if the girls really needed anything.

As they headed east through the woods behind the house, Dave tried to begin a conversation with Marissa. "So tell me a bit about how you two ended up here alone?"

He asked for a couple of reasons. He was curious but really he found himself wanting to look at Marissa more. If she was speaking, it was only polite to look at her while she spoke.

"Sure. It will help pass the time, right?" Marissa offered. Dave just smiled back at her. She was finding it difficult to keep her mind off the feeling of this young man's hands on hers a short time ago. She had felt something she'd never felt before and it scared her. She made sure Kat walked between the two of them, for the time being.

"It's not a long story," Kat offered. "They left to be part of the Occupier protest in Toronto and we haven't heard from them since the phones went offline."

"Okay, short and to the point. Got it," Dave said, looking down at Kat. The knapsack on her back was a little over-sized for her small frame but she had insisted, stating that it carried everything she needed and she couldn't pack 'any more economically'—her wording, exactly.

"So, what do you think happened Kat?" Dave asked her while he was watching Marissa look up into the brightly lit morning. The sun shining off her winter-pale skin made her look angelic, he thought. "O, god! What am I thinking," he said out loud.

"What?" Kat asked him, looking up at him, confused by the statement.

Dave told himself, you need a quick recovery; think fast buddy.

"Um, sorry, Kat. My mind just wandered, ah, for a moment," he replied slowly, giving his mind time to come up with something more credible and less embarrassing than 'I was gawking at your gorgeous sister'. "I was just thinking about that discussion we had regarding your knapsack, um, and how concerned I was about the size. I finally think there's a compromise we can, ah, agree to. Are you willing to listen?" he asked, thinking I hope this doesn't sound overly stupid.

"Sure, what kind of compromise?" Kat asked suspiciously, having already stated her intention to be self-reliant.

"How about we switch when you get tired of that big thing, okay? My pack is much lighter. You can carry yours all the way or we can switch sometime. But only if you want to, deal?" he asked, offering his hand to seal the deal.

"I think I can live with that," Kat replied. She spit into her palm and quickly grabbed Dave's hand, shaking it up and down once.

"That's so lovely," Marissa said, as she looked at Dave with her sincerest smile.

Dave just mumbled a response as he grinned back at Marissa.

"Oh, brother," Kat exclaimed. To herself, she thought, you too as so obvious! She knew better than to embarrass her sister like that though. Let's see how this goes, she thought. She asked Dave a question, "Do you like the Jays or Leafs, Dave?"

She looked up at her sister as she asked the question. Marissa's eyes widened at the question and glanced down at her sister, a sly smile beginning to develop on her face. Kat just winked at her sister as Dave responded positively. Gotcha, Kat thought; you owe me one Marissa.

April 3, 10:00 a.m.

"Okay kids, there are two ways we can do this. First," Sam began as he sat with Ranjeet and Chandra back in the front room of the bed and breakfast they had been living in, "I can walk back and get Caera then bring her here. There are a couple of issues with that, not least of which is the fact that all the medicine and first aid gear that she would need are at her house. He paused to take a deep breath before making his somewhat riskier suggestion, "So, we're probably going to have to get you back somehow, which is the other way."

Chandra and Ranjeet began speaking to each other in a language Sam didn't recognize. He took the opportunity of their private conversation to look about the room. It appeared as if they had been living in that front room for some time, but it made sense. It was close to the kitchen, a bathroom, and had a couch large enough for the two of them to curl up on. With Ranjeet appearing as weak as he did, restricting their living space was expected.

The area hosted a large stone fireplace that still had a good size fire burning. It warmed the room considerably. Sam took off his sweat-shirt and placed it in his lap. He needed to think of a way to transport Ranjeet back to Caera. He noticed that Ranjeet's voice was getting increasingly louder and persistent, and then it stopped.

Chandra's voice broke Sam's thoughts, "We are sorry for speaking privately but we hope you understand. We would like to try and get to this friend of yours and see if she can help us."

She didn't look very sure about this so Sam responded smiling. "Okay then, Chandra, you and I have to try and find something we can transport Ranjeet in. It should be something with wheels. If we are unlucky and can't find anything, I can make a travois."

"A what?" Chandra asked, knowing she had heard the word but couldn't recall the definition.

"A travois. It's a Native-designed way of transporting belongings," Sam began. "Basically, it's a couple of long poles that can be strapped together at one end. They then form a wedge out with some type of material across the poles so that items can be placed on them." Sam attempted to show the general shape with his hands.

"We could then pull him while he rested in it like a stretcher. Various Native groups on the plains used them. Sometimes the travois would also serve as their teepee, or the other way around," Sam explained.

"Oh, I think I remember seeing them in a movie or two," she responded, furrowing her brow as she tried to picture the device.

"Probably, if we can't find anything with wheels I'll fashion one. The trip wouldn't be as quick, that's all." Sam thought for a moment before rising to begin scanning the neighbourhood. "Why don't you two pack whatever you need while I go look for something to help".

Chandra pushed herself up and moved forward to give Sam a hug. "Thank you, so much Mr. Gregory."

"Please call me Sam and it's not a problem," he replied. He stood back and looked down at Chandra's midsection. "You're pregnant?" he asked, noticing her somewhat expanding belly for the first time.

"Yes, due in about four or five months," she answered, rubbing her tummy.

"Gonna have a son!" Ranjeet exclaimed, and then doubled over as intestinal pain shot through him.

Chandra tried to hide the growing look of fear and concern on her face as she turned back to Sam, "Yes, I'll pack a few things but we really don't have much. We were only planning on being away for two days. I can come help you look in a few minutes."

"Take your time," Sam replied as he opened the door and walked out.

I have to get both of them back to Caera, he thought. She can't have a baby out here on her own, with her husband so sick. He tried to search his mind for what someone might have in their yard to help transport Ranjeet, when Chandra came out.

"Ranjeet's fallen asleep so I can help. You know, I was thinking, one of the neighbours was in a wheelchair. I used to see the husband out pushing the wife almost every day, regardless of the weather. They left quite a while ago but maybe there's an extra one around their house. What do you think? I don't know why I didn't think of it earlier," she said, rebuking herself.

"I think it's worth a try. All I've seen is that tricycle," Sam said, pointing to the yard across the street.

Besides the tricycle lying on its side, there was a small bicycle with training wheels, a child's baseball glove, and a small hockey stick spread out on the front lawn.

"A young family lived there. They left a few weeks after we arrived," Chandra added with more than just a hint of sadness and a slight frown. "The little boy was named Farmer. He used to ride that bike up and down the driveway-" she trailed off as she began to tear up again. "I'm so sorry, Sam. It's just been so," she paused, not sure what words to use and wiping at the tears that began to roll down her cheeks.

"It's okay, I understand. It's been tough on everyone. Let's go see about a wheelchair," Sam replied, wanting to keep her mind occupied on something other than the negative aspects of her situation.

After peering through only their second window, they were rewarded. There in the middle of the hallway was a wheelchair. They checked every window and door for a way in but all were firmly secured. With a touch of remorse, Sam broke a window and let himself in.

Chandra walked the wheelchair back while Sam looked for something to use to board up the broken window. With little effort, he found a hammer, nails, and some boards in the garage of the house.

He nailed the boards into place over the break. He did this out of guilt and to keep wildlife from getting inside the house. He also left a short note on the kitchen table explaining why the window was broken and the wheelchair gone. He didn't know if anyone would ever see the note, but for now he believed it was the right thing to do.

By the time he got back to Chandra and Ranjeet, they were waiting by the road. Ranjeet was sitting comfortably in the wheelchair with a sports bag in his lap. There were two medium-sized overnight bags as well, one slung over Chandra's left shoulder and another hung on the back of the wheelchair.

Chandra was standing behind Ranjeet, one hand on his shoulder as she bent over whispering in his ear. He smiled slightly and nodded his head. Sam slowed his approach to give them a moment's more privacy.

Tux, who had been sitting watching them all, approached and jumped into Ranjeet's lap. He looked up at Ranjeet and Chandra, then curled up on top of the sports bag and began dozing.

Chandra looked up, saw Sam approaching and smiled. "I think we're all ready. All three of us," Chandra stated, smiling down at the cat. She squeezed her husband's shoulder gently, kissed his ear, and began pushing the wheelchair towards Sam.

"Can I carry something or help in any way?" Sam offered.

144

"You're already carrying a big pack. I'm sure in a little while, I'll ask for a break," Chandra replied. "Thank you though. You've already given us both some hope," she replied, touching his forearm gently in friendly appreciation.

"Not a problem and please let me know if I can help at all," Sam answered in return. "It took me about two hours or so of steady walking. So we might be looking at about three to get back. Now, has everyone gone to the bathroom before we leave?" Sam asked, in as light a mood as possible.

Ranjeet and Chandra both chuckled. "Lead on, good man," Ranjeet insisted in his hoarse tone. He looked down at the cat and just shook his head, placing his right hand on the sleeping cat and rubbing between his ears. Tux just turned his head a little in response and kept on dozing.

The four of them began their journey back towards Shane and Caera's house, Chandra pushing Ranjeet and the sleeping Tux, Sam keeping pace on their left.

"So, what brings you to this part of the world," Sam asked as they began their trek south.

"Would you like the long version or the short one?" Chandra offered, looking up at him.

"Well, we have a couple of hours ahead of us. Whatever you feel most comfortable sharing," he replied.

The collapse of the dollar might be a particularly trying catastrophe of its own or occur as part of an even larger collapse of civilization. It might merely mark a turning away from the excesses of paper money or be a milepost on the way to a maelstrom. None of this is inevitable but all of it is possible.

Social and financial collapses have happened many times but are easily ignored or forgotten. Yet history does not forget, nor do complex systems refrain from doing what they are wont to do. Complex systems begin on a benign organizing principle and end by absorbing all available energy while destroying the system itself.

James Rickards, 2011
Currency Wars: The Making of the Next Global Crisis

April 3, 12:30 p.m.

"Good afternoon sleepyhead," Shane whispered to the top of his wife's head as he leaned over their bed.

Caera was still curled up, enjoying the warmth of the sun shining in through the window and heating the dark comforter she was laying beneath. She had taken all the covers and piled them on top of her, only leaving the top of her head exposed to the light. "What time is it?" she asked, popping her head out from under the covers, her eyes trying to adjust to the bright light.

"A little past noon," Shane answered as he threw open the window, letting some fresh air into the room. "And, it's a gloriously warm April day with the thermometer reading twenty degrees already. I'm sure it's another record for the books."

"How long have you been up, honey?" Caera asked, stretching her arms over her head and slowly rolling out from under the comforter.

"I don't know. I guess I was up about seven or so. I wanted to start working outside," Shane replied, returning to the bed and sitting on the edge near her.

"Why didn't you wake me earlier?" she asked as she walked to her dresser.

"I learned my lesson about waking you early in our marriage, if you remember," he answered, patting her behind.

"I'm getting a lot better," she insisted. They both recognised that Caera needed at least a good nine hours of sleep. She was a true bear otherwise.

"Yes, you are," he answered, slipping his hand on the inside of her right thigh, just above the knee, letting it drift upwards.

"Can I help you, sir?" she asked, stopping his hand before it got much further.

"Maybe later," he suggested, winking at her. "Come on outside when you get dressed. I need some advice on how to proceed with this latest project."

"Is there any coffee left?" Caera asked her husband, hoping the answer was yes.

"I'm afraid not, early bird gets the worm," Shane replied apologetically. Then after a moment's pause he continued, "Would you like me to make some more for you? I've got a bit of hot water left and I didn't use the whole day's ration of coffee," he finished, winking at her.

"That would be lovely," Caera replied, picking up a pillow and throwing it at him. "Did Sam leave yet?" she enquired, turning to open a dresser drawer.

"Yep, we said goodbye first thing this morning shortly after I got up. It's too bad too, it's been quite useful to have him around all these years," Shane responded.

"Absolutely, I don't know what shape we'd be in if he hadn't helped us. Did he mention if he'd be back at all?" Caera asked as she began looking through her clothes.

"Not for a while, I think. He did warn me that we might see some family members some time. But, I'm a bit doubtful after so long. We've not seen anyone else for at least two months."

"Too bad," Caera said as she slipped out of her nightclothes. "Twenty degrees, you said?"

"Yep," Shane replied, enjoying the view of his tall, athletic wife changing.

Caera moved some clothes around and then took out a pair of shorts and an old t-shirt. "Is there fresh water in the bathroom, honey?" she asked, slipping a University of Guelph t-shirt on over her head.

"Just brought some in," Shane replied.

"You're a doll," she purred, as she leaned over and kissed him on the nose. "Coffee?"

"I'll get right to it," Shane stated as he rose and left the bedroom. "Sam left us his garden to take advantage of, remember? Did you want to go have a look?"

"Sure, right after my coffee," she reminded him. "Actually," she paused, thinking about it. "Let's head over as soon as the coffee's ready. I think I remember how he has it all laid out. We're okay to expand into his yard and greenhouse? You're sure?" she asked as she entered the kitchen.

"Yes, Sam was very specific. We have full access to the garden and greenhouse. If anyone from his family shows up, we would obviously cede the space to them. Or, if he comes back down before the fall harvest, he'd simply ask to take enough of the food to get him through the winter. Don't you remember we talked about this a couple of weeks ago?" Shane answered his wife's question and then opened up the door to their deck.

He stepped outside in order to retrieve a large black, vinyl bag; this was their solar water heater. When left in the sun, the black vinyl absorbed the sun's rays. The heat was passed on to the water inside and they had hot water. Shane wished he had about a dozen more of these camp showers that he had purchased from Canadian Tire a number of years ago for a camping trip. It was one of the productive items he and Caera had kept with them when they moved.

"Yes. I remember," Caera replied, sitting down at the kitchen table to prepare a couple of pieces of fresh bread to eat as they walked. "I just want to make sure," she finished, patting her husband on the behind as he walked by.

Shane finished with the coffee press, pouring his wife a fresh cup of coffee. "We're down to about six tins. Do we start going every two weeks?" he asked. "It will last twice as long."

"Do we go to a month?" she countered, raising her eyebrows.

"I don't think I could go a whole month," was Shane's response.

"When you were younger, you couldn't go a whole twelve hours," she teased him.

As he was about to hand off the coffee to her, there was a knock on the door. Shane spilled the coffee all over his hand as he flinched with the knock. "Fuck!" he swore. He quickly grabbed the cup with the other hand and placed it on the counter as he stuck his stinging hand in the bowl of cold water sitting in the sink.

"Sounds like the door," he said between gritted teeth.

Caera tried to hide her grin. She knew the water could get quite hot in the solar heater, particularly with mid-summer sun. But she also knew that it would not scald so early in the day. Hurt? Yes, but it would take most of the day in full sun to get hot enough to do any harm this time of the year. She peered through the front window to see who it was.

It was Sam and two strangers, one being in a wheelchair. She immediately opened the front door and greeted Sam.

"Caera, I have a friend who needs your attention," was Sam's response as a cat ran past her into the house.

The primary question is whether we want our future to be shaped by disaster or by design. The set of predicaments and problems that we now face are very different from the conditions of the past 20 years and therefore present a solid challenge to the existing status quo. Those currently wielding power and influence are most likely to defend the status quo, raising the risk that our future will consist more of disaster than design. Further, abrupt changes have the unfortunate tendency of escaping notice by the majority of people, who have been conditioned to expect that the future will resemble the past. This is a perfectly valid assumption for ordinary moments, but it is a liability during extraordinary times.

Chris Martenson, 2011
The Crash Course

October 15, 10:00 p.m.

Mac backed Laz's car as close as possible to his unconscious classmate. Ernie loaded her gear into her car then came back to help Mac move Laz into the passenger side of his car.

"What makes you say the military will be here?" Ernie asked Mac, some of the colour starting to return to her slightly freckled cheeks.

"I'm pretty sure that crash was caused by an unmanned drone coming down. I don't know a lot about drones but I would think there was a built-in GPS unit. If they don't know why already, they're going to want to determine why it came down and that means getting to it. And, probably sooner rather than later," Mac explained as Ernie carefully stabilised Laz's leg while Mac slid his arms under Laz and lifted him, supporting his head and most of his weight. Like this, they moved Laz, Mac dragging him to the passenger side of the car while Ernie made sure his injured leg was protected.

It took them a few minutes, but they managed to move Laz without incident.

"You lead," Mac said to Ernie. "Let's at least get out of the park as quick as we can. Once we lock up, we can chat about what our next step is."

"Shouldn't it be to an emergency room at a hospital?" Ernie asked, motioning towards Laz.

"I'm not sure. We've just witnessed the crash of a Canadian military drone not long after our government has denied the existence of such equipment for domestic surveillance. Do you remember the hullabaloo with the last budget and the attempt to have military purchases made public, and-" Mac abruptly stopped talking and turned his left ear towards the west. "Do you hear that?" he asked Ernie.

"There's something coming this way," Ernie gasped, fear entering her voice again.

"Turn the car lights off, quick," Mac ordered as he dashed for the driver's side of Laz's car, hitting the lights and then stepping up on the bumper to try and get a better idea of how close, what he was beginning to believe was a helicopter was to them.

Ernie had quickly turned her own car's lights off and then ran back to join Mac. "Is it another drone?" she asked, standing right beside him, looking unsure of what to do.

"No, I think it might be a helicopter. Do you know the route well enough to get us to the front gate using just the light we have from the moon?" Mac asked, looking down into Ernie's dark brown eyes. He could see that she was scared by the way she looked to him for assurance. "Hell of a way to sober up real fast isn't it?" he joked as he jumped down from the bumper. "We'll be fine, don't worry," he added, placing a hand on her shoulder and squeezing gently..

"Somebody's buying somebody a drink after this," Ernie replied. "And I'm having a double!"

"You lead the way. We'll be okay, just get us to the front gate," Mac encouraged her as he led her back to her car. He could imagine the helicopter closing in on their location, its searchlight combing the various coulees as it approached. He figured that they had less than a minute to get going. If they could avoid the spotlight on their way out they might not get tangled up in any military red tape. Besides, Mac thought, I'm not done here. "Don't take any chances with anything. If the military show up, don't try to run," he instructed Ernie.

It was a nerve-wracking ten minutes to get to the front gate. Ernie quickly unlocked the gate and let Mac and Laz out. She left the lock and key hanging on the gate for Mac, who locked up as soon as her car was clear. He could begin to hear Laz coming to as he walked back to the car. Ernie was standing beside Laz, checking on him and reassuring him that he was fine.

"What happened?" he asked groggily. "Last thing I remember I was sitting at the campfire and eating sushi. "What the hell happened to my leg," he shouted, distress finally entering his voice, as he noticed his injury for the first time.

"I'll explain everything when we're on our way out of here, Laz. It's not as bad as it looks," Mac said, putting his hand under Laz's forearm hanging out the car window and gently placed it back in his lap. "Please keep limbs inside the vehicle at all times, sir," Mac continued. "You had a little accident with a, model plane, that's all."

Laz looked at him, unsure of what to say. "Not as bad as it looks? I've got a fucking piece of metal sticking out of my leg! Not as bad as it looks?!" He looked down at his leg and then up at Ernie and Mac. Ernie just shrugged her shoulders and looked to the sky, pretending not to know anything.

"I'll explain what happened once we get going, Laz," Mac assured his classmate. He then turned to Ernie, "You need to lead us towards Lethbridge," Mac insisted.

"Sure thing," Ernie responded. "The Chinook Regional Hospital is on Nineteenth Street South. Do you know where that is?" Ernie asked as she got into her car and started it.

"I've got a pretty good idea. You lead the way, though. Have you got a cell phone?" he asked, as he made his way back to Laz's car. The chopper appeared to be hovering somewhere; its buzz was not getting closer or fading.

"Give me the number quickly and then go," he urged, they needed to get going. Ernie shouted out her number and they both climbed into their cars.

Pulling his phone out, Mac punched in Ernie's number and started the car. She answered on the third ring. "Have you got hands-free?" Mac asked her as soon as she answered.

"Yeah, I do," Ernie replied. "Listen, in case we lose touch. We're starting on Highway 500 and will take this up to Highway 501, then west on Highway 501 to the town of Milk River. That's where we meet Highway 4. It runs north into Lethbridge. We've got about a fifty or sixty minute drive ahead of us. Will Laz be okay?"

"Highways 500 to 501 to 4, got it, and Laz will be fine," Mac said, finally letting out a breath that he seemed to have been holding since this whole situation began. "Hang on a sec, Ernie, I've got to put my cell on speakerphone," he instructed as he tried to find the right buttons in what little moonlight penetrated into the car.

Ernie could hear him fumbling around as she began driving away from the park.

They hadn't gone three minutes down the highway when Ernie saw what looked like a truck in the middle of the road just ahead. "Mac, are you there?" she asked, beginning to feel her heart racing. "We appear to have a little problem up ahead," Ernie warned as she began to slow her car down. It was the military erecting a checkpoint on the highway. The blockade appeared to be only half constructed, with a couple of personnel moving barriers into place still.

"Guys," she muttered into the air, "any suggestions?"

"You go through. Don't worry about us," Mac replied. "Just say you're on your way back from somewhere. I'll think of something for us." Mac had no idea what he was going to do. If they looked deep enough into his records, they might arrest him on the spot. It was too late for him to turn around, however.

"I've got it," Ernie said. "We are on our way back from camping at Cypress Hill. It's a provincial park on the border with Saskatchewan and it hasn't been closed yet. That will explain the camping gear and food."

"Brilliant. We're with you but had separate cars," Mac said. He looked at Laz. Now that he was conscious, the piece of metal sticking out of his leg had his full attention. It was obvious that he was fighting some significant pain every time he moved.

"Ernie? Are you ready?" Mac said as he saw someone approach her car.

"As ready as I'll ever be," she replied, trying not to sound overly unsure of herself as they ended their phone connection.

"How about you, pal?" Mac asked Laz. He looked over briefly at his classmate. Laz looked fine, apart from the piece of metal sticking out of his leg.

"Yep, as long as I don't have to get out of the car," he grunted back. He was trying to focus on remaining still. As long as he didn't move too much he could hang on until they reached Lethbridge, even though it was a good sixty minutes away. He just couldn't move, otherwise he was in excruciating pain. Amazingly, the wound did not appear to be bleeding too much at all.

"We have to hide that metal," Mac stated and began looking around in the back seat for something to mask the metal sticking out of Laz's leg. "Here," he handed Laz his MacBook. "Start up iTunes and then get a movie started. Hide the metal with the computer. Here comes somebody."

Mac took a few deep, deliberate breaths to calm his rising anxiety then hit the automatic window opener on his driver's side. Laz made sure the laptop he was holding obscured the piece of metal protruding from his leg. "Let's hope it's our lucky night," Mac said. He quickly turned on the voice recorder application of his phone and then placed it by the open window on the car's dashboard.

"Hi. Is there a problem?" Mac asked the person walking up to his car.

The young lady appeared to be about nineteen or twenty. "Just a moment please, sir," she stated, then stepped back a few metres to meet someone else walking towards them. They began a conversation over the logistics of the road block.

"She's a corporal, see the two stripes, and the one who joined her is a sergeant, first class, three stripes on top and two stripes underneath," Mac whispered to Laz. Mac could hear some chatter on the walkie-talkies the two were wearing. He made out Writing-On-Stone Park among the words being relayed. He took another long, deep breath and let it out slowly.

"Sir, we've had some unusual activity in the area tonight," began the sergeant, "if you don't mind, could you please step out of the car for a moment and open your trunk."

"Um, sure," he snuck a glance at Laz who was looking dumbfounded at the request; eyes wide open, mouthing 'Fuck'.

As Mac got out he could see that Ernie had to do the same just in front of them. He could hear her explaining that they were together and just coming home from camping. The sergeant joined Mac at the back of the car while the corporal remained at the open driver's side door, scanning the backseat with her flashlight.

She shone the light directly towards Laz in the front, "Please put the computer down, sir, and step out on your side."

At the same time, it's important to recognise that there is only so much that individuals can do on their own. Some of the disruptions we may be facing would not be of short duration. A few weeks' worth of stored food and water, though essential, will be of only temporary help. Over longer time frames, our most valuable personal assets will be functioning local communities composed of people who despite their differences, are willing and able to work together to solve problems and maximize opportunities.

The maintenance of social cohesion must be our single highest priority in a future of mounting economic and environmental challenges.

Richard Heinberg, 2011
The End of Growth

April 3, 3:00 pm

Once again, Sam found himself sitting in his home, only this time he had company. He and Chandra had left Ranjeet in Caera's care and, on Caera's advice, Sam was keeping Chandra occupied. Chandra sat across from him at his kitchen table, the notes to his family still spread out on the table beside the front door and close to Chandra's elbow.

"Your Dad? Is he close by?" Chandra enquired after noticing the letters and picking one up.

"Hmm, long story," Sam began. "Um, he, ah-"

"I'm sorry. I don't mean to pry," Chandra interrupted, placing the envelope back on the table. She bent her head to the side and grabbed the long black strands of her hair hanging down onto the floor. Sam hoped the floor was clean. Chandra had a rather large hair elastic in her other hand and made a couple of loops in her hair and then tied it up, swinging it behind her.

"No, um, it's fine, really. Um, he's with my mum in Toronto. She's very ill and not able to travel," Sam offered. He knew it was not the entire truth but it was enough to satisfy the question without getting into a long story.

"I'm sorry," Chandra said, feeling guilty for asking something that was obviously personal for Sam. "I'll stop being nosy."

"It's not a prob-" Sam was interrupted by a knock on the door. "That could be Caera or Shane," he said to Chandra, getting up to answer the door.

Sam opened the door only to be shocked by the presence of three people, one of them his brother, Dave.

"Brudda!" Dave said, embracing his older brother in a bear hug.

Sam was speechless. He was ecstatic to see his brother after all this time, however he was a bit taken aback by the fact that he had two others in tow, and one of them a young girl no more than ten.

"Sam, this is Marissa and her little sister, Kat," Dave stated, introducing his two companions.

"Little?" stated Kat, looking up at Dave, raising one eyebrow slightly. "How about younger!"

***

"I haven't shared everything with Marissa and Kat," Dave said to his brother Sam, as they sat alone on Sam's porch. The girls, Chandra, Marissa, and Kat, were busy exploring the area close to the lake. They had been chatting since the two younger girls had arrived and could see that Sam and Dave needed to have a few moments of privacy.

Sitting in an old Adirondack chair on Sam's front porch, Dave was beginning to feel the stress of the last few days and rolled his head left and then right.

"Oh, do you have to do that!" Sam said to his brother, hearing the 'cracking' of Dave's neck, not once but twice. "It's always sent shivers right down my back. What else do you know?" Sam asked, beginning to wonder how all this news, and all these people, were going to alter his plans.

"Sorry," Dave apologized, "I've been sleeping on the ground the past few nights and have just hiked about a hundred kilometres after a relatively slothful lifestyle. I'm not feeling the best. Look," Dave began in all seriousness, "I've only told the girls about the security forces kettling everyone into the area around Queen's Park. The rest of Jim's news is a bit more troubling. He said there were two things that puzzled him. First, it looked as though the security forces were having difficulty maintaining power. And, I don't mean authoritarian power, but electrical power. Toronto had fairly regular electricity until about a month ago, and then it started experiencing longer and longer blackouts. Jim said that about two weeks ago Toronto lost all power and it never returned."

"Wow, I wonder what has happened?" Sam asked, not expecting Toronto to have lost its power also.

"There was no power anywhere except what the military and police could generate with gas-powered backups," Dave continued. "The other odd observation that Jim made was that it appeared that there was less security patrolling each day during the last week or so that he was there. He wondered if maybe they were evacuating because of the loss of power," Dave offered

"Who knows, but if Toronto has lost all power and the military and police are evacuating, you know it's not good," Sam replied, looking out over his neighbourhood as he tried to ponder what it all meant, and what might happen next.

"Jim also shared that as security lessened more and more people were beginning to migrate out of the Toronto area. As patrols shrank in size and frequency, people were taking their chances on the streets because the markets were closed more often and when they did open the food was severely rationed. Many were arrested, but then Jim said it appeared as if security was just absent in some places. The day that he made it out, he said about a hundred people just walked past a security gate when no one was around. He said it was bizarre given what had been happening up until that point."

"I don't know what any of it means but I was headed north this morning. I think you and I need to head up that way again, and soon," Sam suggested to his brother.

"What about everyone else?" Dave asked, a bit shocked that his brother would just leave.

"My place up north isn't meant for everybody that's shown up, Dave," Sam said, recognizing that his brother was more like his sister in altruistic tendencies.

"It's the right thing to do!" Dave responded immediately.

"Is it?" Sam asked, and not rhetorically.

"What do you mean?" Dave was sounding more incredulous with each sentence.

"Take emotions out of this, first," Sam warned his brother.

"Sam we're humans, we are emotional! You can't just leave everyone," Dave challenged.

"Yes, but you know as well as I do that giving in to your reptilian instincts blocks out the rational part of your brain," Sam advised his younger brother, trying to calm him and keep him thinking logically and not emotionally.

"You know what Susie would say," Dave countered, beginning to sense where their conversation might lead.

"I know exactly what Susie would say but I'm not prepared to take so many people under my wing. My vision was for our family, not a group of strangers brought together by an unthinkable situation. I'm not prepared to try and support so many people. People we don't even really know," Sam argued. This was the perennial debate between he and Susie; alone or together, together or alone, which was best? Would survival be maximized within a group or outside of a group?

"I can't believe you!" Dave pushed. He was getting upset and fought to control himself. He looked away from his brother, towards the lake. He could see the two women and young girl walking along the lake's western shoreline. The sun was beginning to dip towards the horizon. Any other time, Dave would have enjoyed the moment but he was in no mood. As the sun began to emerge from behind some clouds, the light reflected off the lake causing him to shield his eyes and for a moment the image of a mushroom cloud seemed to emerge. He was struck by an appalling thought and then an epiphany.

"What if everyone were in danger?" he asked, standing on the edge of Sam's porch. He turned around so suddenly that he startled Tux who was sleeping by Sam's feet. Tux looked up annoyed, but then put his head back down and was asleep again in seconds.

"What do you mean?" Sam responded, not knowing where his brother was going with the conversation.

Dave retreated to his seat and sat down. He leaned forward towards his brother, resting his elbows on his knees and clasping his hands together. Looking at his brother and being as serious as he could, he began to outline his thoughts regarding a couple of black swans. "I've had a lot of time to think about what Jim told me with respect to the situation in Toronto. There are two possible scenarios that worry me with the loss of power being so widespread."

Sam listened attentively to his brother, but in the back of his mind he was beginning to grow worried himself. He had growing concerns about the millions of people in Toronto migrating out in all directions and on the verge of possible starvation. Dave, however, offered something Sam hadn't thought about.

"If power's out everywhere, what happens with the Darlington and Pickering nuclear power stations?" Dave posed to his brother, concern really beginning to show on his face.

Sam's southern home was only about sixty kilometres from two of Ontario's three nuclear plants. A power outage for an extended period of time would create problems for the nuclear plants, Sam was certain.

"I never thought about that scenario," Sam admitted. "I've always been more concerned with the impact of resource depletion on sociopolitical systems. I've never really thought about the loss of our electrical grid and all the consequences that would follow."

"Boy, boy, boy dear, what are ya, bloody stupid?" Dave said, mimicking their late Zio Giovanni, their mother's brother.

***

Everyone had gathered in Sam's living room. He looked around and thought, ten hours ago I was all on my own, now there are eight of us. And a cat, he reminded himself, looking over at Kat who had Tux curled up in her lap, asleep.

Shane, Caera, Kat, and Tux shared his couch.

At one end of the couch, Chandra was sitting on one of Sam's oak kitchen chairs. Beside her was Ranjeet, sitting in the wheelchair. Caera had helped to stabilize him but she had no idea what was wrong with him. He seemed to be having difficulty remaining awake.

Dave had just finished sharing what little information he had about events in Toronto. Sitting in the loveseat across from the couch, he was having difficulty keeping still.

Sam could see that he was also having difficulty keeping his gaze away from his new friend, Marissa. He'd seen that look on his brother's face before, that of a lovesick puppy dog. Marissa was not helping the situation. She sat beside Dave and kept glancing at him, smiling when their eyes caught each other's. This could complicate matters, Sam thought.

"I think our choices are limited. This area would be perfect except for one major unknown," Sam began.

"What would that be?" Shane asked him, concern rising in his voice.

"Well," Sam began, taking a deep breath and sighing, knowing that this conversation was not going to be easy, especially for Shane.

"If the situation is as chaotic as reported to Dave, we all may want to consider distancing ourselves from this area."

"Why?" Shane asked. "We've always agreed on what an ideal location this area is." He was confused and beginning to get defensive.

"All things being equal, it is," Sam agreed, trying to defuse some of Shane's concern and rising emotion. "But things aren't equal anymore based on what Dave's reported. If the information is correct, that even the military and police are having power supply issues and the Greater Toronto Area has lost all power as well, then one concern would be the nuclear reactors not sixty kilometres away. Without power for an extended period of time, I don't know how stable the reactors can be kept. Have they been shut down safely? I don't know, and what happens if they haven't? Or, what happens with all the waste products they store on site? Does everyone remember Fukushima, Chernobyl, and Three Mile Island?"

"Yeah, but Japan's reactor was damaged by a huge tsunami," Shane countered, trying desperately to justify his home being safe.

"Absolutely," Sam acknowledged. "We also know about the human errors that led to the situation being worse than it should have been, and the lies that were being told repeatedly by Japanese leaders about their clean-up and control of the reactor during the following years. Regardless, I know enough to know that any nuclear reactor still relies on backup generators during power outages and I don't think they're designed for extended periods of time. Plus, if the situation is such that the fuel and waste products are not monitored twenty-four hours a day, then who knows what might happen. Human error, unintended consequences, and unknown variables have all contributed to every previous nuclear accident that the planet has experienced, at least that I'm aware of.

"If our entire electrical grid is down for an extended period of time, I really believe we are in for widespread chaos, to say the least. Heaven knows how many nuclear reactors and waste facilities there are just on this half of the continent. If power is out as extensively as it was during the 2003 blackout, then we could have dozens of reactors and waste facilities about to radiate their local communities, putting tens of millions of people at risk."

A hush fell over the group and Sam watched the various reactions. Shane had a hand resting on his wife's knee. Caera placed one of her hands over her husband's and shifted a little closer to him on the couch. Sam could see that her eyes were beginning to fill with tears.

Kat stroked Tux a bit more energetically and looked at her sister for assurance. Tux just slept on.

Marissa looked back at her younger sister but her hand, unconscious to her, reached out towards Dave. Dave, who had been looking at his brother, felt Marissa's hand as it barely touched his own. Sam noted that Dave's gaze remained on him but he slid his hand over Marissa's. A slight grin came on Dave's face, and he coloured. Totally smitten my brother is, Sam thought.

Last he looked at Chandra and Ranjeet. Tears were also rolling down Chandra's cheeks as she squeezed her husband's hand. Ranjeet appeared to have fallen asleep. Only time would tell if his body could recover from whatever ailed him, and would he survive such a trip?

It was Caera who broke the silence. "What option do we have?" She wiped at her tears but they kept coming.

"I have some land up north. It will mean a lot of work for everyone. To be honest," Sam paused, thinking about how quickly his life had shifted, again. "I wasn't planning on there being so many of us. There'll be a lot of work at the beginning, but if we all pitch in I think we could be okay there. We could always come back south if things ever return to 'normal.'"

"God, I don't know Sam," Shane said, shaking his head. "We've invested everything we have here. We've got nothing else." He looked at his wife and took both her hands in his. Tears were rolling steadily down her cheeks.

Looking directly at Shane, Sam responded, "Honestly my place up north is not prepared for our numbers. It will take a lot of effort by everybody to make it support all of us. But I know you and Caera know what to do to help make it a sustainable location."

"When would you want to leave? I'm worried about Ranjeet," Chandra asked, worried that her husband was in no state to make such a journey.

"The sooner the better, to be honest," Dave offered, looking at Marissa and Kat.

Kat gave a half grin and nodded her head, looking forward to the adventure that awaited her on the road. Marissa, however, was on the verge of a panic attack. She could feel the adrenaline begin to speed her heart and quicken her breathing. Slow it down, she told herself, before you have a meltdown in front of everyone.

"Look, everyone," Sam began, trying to make eye contact with each person as he spoke, "I will be as straightforward as I can with what information I have. History and prehistory are littered with examples of social and political collapse. Some of these collapses have happened relatively quickly due to environmental catastrophes, while others have happened relatively slowly as an empire found it harder and harder to afford the security to protect itself from competitors. I've personally felt that our globalised world has been heading for some type of collapse for almost a decade. It is not necessarily something bad, it is just something different. History doesn't necessarily repeat itself because of all the different variables in both time and culture, but the present certainly can rhyme with the past. If our government has lost control, for whatever reason, then we can expect some negative consequences, not least of which will be the lawlessness that could arise due to the lack of food and millions of starving people heading out of the Toronto area. I am not trying to frighten anyone. I am just trying to be realistic.

"I was heading north this morning, even before the spectre of total grid failure and I feel a need to get away from the area as soon as possible. Obviously, the decision to join me up north should be discussed more privately with each of your partners. It's already getting late so no one is going anywhere today. I suggest we meet again in an hour or so and share decisions or thoughts."

And with that, Sam stood and began striding for the front door.

"Sam, wait up," Dave called, as he patted Marissa's hand. "Chat with Kat, I'll be back in a few minutes," he assured her.

Before the brothers could open the front door, Caera joined them. "Guys, let me join you for a moment," Caera began, opening the door for them and then following them outside. She moved away from the door after closing it and looked at both Sam and Dave, "I don't think Ranjeet is in any condition to travel. Not for the distance and time you're suggesting."

Sam looked back at her and sighed, "I thought that might be the case but thank you for confirming it for me, Caera."

"I know it complicates matters, but I don't think he'll be able to travel for some time," she finished, turning to go back into Sam's house and begin a difficult discussion with her husband.

"Well?" Sam asked, looking at his brother.

"I don't know, things are pretty complicated now aren't they?" Dave asked somewhat rhetorically. "If we have one member who can't travel, do we risk the rest of the group for the chance that he might recover? This is kind of like the Kobayahsi Maru test on Star Trek, no possibility of coming out without a significant loss of some kind."

"I'm wondering if we need to split up, send some up now and others follow later. What do you think?" Sam asked his brother. A plan was beginning to germinate in his mind but it would mean splitting up with his brother who had just arrived.

"Well," Dave began, looking at his older brother with a growing idea as to what he might suggest, "I'm assuming that you and I would have to take separate groups as I can't imagine others in our group have the training in survival skills that you and I have."

"Agreed," Sam responded. "If Ranjeet can't travel, Chandra's not going to be leaving."

"And, by the sounds of it, Caera would likely choose to remain and continue care for Ranjeet and monitor Chandra's pregnancy, which means Shane would choose to stay as well. That leaves just you and me with Marissa and Kat," Dave concluded.

"And?" Sam probed, nodding his agreement.

"You think I should take Marissa and Kat north while you remain behind with the others," Dave finished with a growing realisation that this course of action might be the wisest.

"I think that sending you north with the two young ladies can serve a couple of purposes. First, you can train them in some important skills during your trek north. You can also start prepping the site for the extensive gardening we're going to have to do to support a much larger group than I had plan-"

The front door opened and Shane walked out, his face revealing the strain of the past hour or so.

"Guys, um, Caera and I have had a chance to chat and, ah, she's determined to stay as long as Ranjeet is unable to travel. Obviously, I'm not going to leave my wife behind," he finished, looking at the two other men.

"We figured as much," Sam replied, placing a reassuring hand on Shane's shoulder. "We think we have a plan that will work and perhaps it's time to share it," Sam said as he patted Shane on the back and began moving for the door. "Come on back in and we'll all discuss it."

The three men reentered Sam's house and joined the rest of the group, interrupting a discussion between Caera and Chandra. Caera was trying to calm Chandra, who was having difficulty holding back her emotions, tears streaming down her face.

Shane caught his wife's eye and through his body language and facial expression asked if everything was okay. She replied positively with a tight nod of her head.

Once again, Sam began the conversation, "Um," he started, then paused, not quite sure how to broach the subject of splitting the group up. "There are a couple of mitigating circumstances that we need to consider before we proceed much further along with this idea of heading north. The most obvious is Ranjeet's illness and Caera's concern about him traveling for an extended time." He looked at Chandra, who seemed to have given up trying to fight the tears and buried her head in her hands. Caera continued to rub her back and assure her things would be fine.

"Dave and I would like to suggest that we send a small group north as soon as possible and begin to prepare the site for all of us, and the others will remain here for the time being until we can get Ranjeet on his feet again." Sam paused to allow the group a moment to ponder the suggestion.

"As Dave and I know the location and have the most experience in traveling through backcountry, it would make the most sense for one of us to lead a small group and the other to remain behind. We're thinking that if Dave heads up tomorrow with Marissa and Kat-"

Once again, Sam was interrupted by a knock on the door. Everyone in the room looked at each other in surprise. Shane quickly looked through a nearby window and announced, "I think it's your sister, guys, and three other-" he stopped cold. "Holy shit, I think one is my Uncle Mac!"

"What?" Sam replied in complete shock, rising from his seat and moving towards the front door at the same time as Shane and Dave. How many times am I going to have to revise my damned plans, Sam asked himself, opeing his front door to greet his sister and her three companions.

Thus ends Book One

I may not know what's right, but I know this can't be it.

Men Without Hats, 1983
Unsatisfaction, Folk of the 80s (Part III)

Passage from Olduvai II

"Where the hell did you get these?" Dave asked his brother as he began shuffling through the pile of papers Sam had just thrown down in front of his brother, Mac and Shane.

"Chandra gave them to me. She found them in Ranjeet's belongings," Sam replied, still in complete disbelief at the content of some of the pages he had perused.

"They look pretty official, Sam. How'd he get a hold of them?" Mac asked, picking up a group of papers that were stapled together.

"Chandra doesn't know so if Ranjeet doesn't regain consciousness, we may never know how he came to possess them. But I agree, they look official," Sam replied, rubbing his scalp in disbelief.

"Did you see this one?" Shane asked, as he handed the group of papers he was holding to Dave.

"Holy shit!" Dave replied as he read the title out loud. "American troops observed amassing on the border between the Great Lakes and Rockies."

"There's a hell of a lot more damning insight into world events than that in this pile, let me tell you," Sam stated, slowly shaking his head. "It appears that some of what has been happening has been planned. Look at this." Sam picked out some papers and placed them on top so everyone could see them. It was an apparent email from the Prime Minister's Office to the Public Safety Minister referencing 'Operation TOR'.

"Operation TOR? What is that?" enquired Shane.

"It appears to be a reference to the Toronto Occupier Riot from my reading," Sam responded. "But I'm puzzled by the fact that the email is dated weeks before the protest even occurred and proposes using an announcement about a terrorist attack on Queen's Park to remove civil liberties."

"Wow! This puts everything in a different light. Do you think we need to rethink our plans?" Dave asked, looking at his brother.

Afterword

In reflecting on why I decided to put the preceding story to print, I realised that there are a number of reasons.

First, since I watched Michael Ruppert's documentary, *Collapse*, almost two years ago, I have spent hundreds of hours reading and researching the thesis he presented: global civilisation will undergo a significant sociopolitical transformation in the not-too-distant future. In the process I have read about Systems Theory and Economics, both fascinating fields, and got back into my graduate work subject, Archaeology. I hope that things do not turn out as badly as Ruppert argues, but the evidence does seem to be supporting his predictions fairly well.

Second, given my concern about Ruppert's argument, I wanted my family to read about some of the issues that are threatening not just our way of life, but our very species. Writing a story and publishing a book seemed like a good way for a number of reasons, not least of which is hopefully the 'pressure' to read my book.

Third, this journey has been cathartic; it has provided an avenue to share some ideas and thoughts so as to reduce my own anxiety somewhat. There are other reasons as well but these are the main ones.

Regardless if you are family or not, I hope you found the story entertaining and the issues compelling enough to look into yourself. Finally, I take responsibility for all mistakes, grammatical, interpretive, and 'factual'.

Thanks to: my wife, Terry, for her endless support and feedback; my two lovely daughters who sort of understand their father's ~~neurosis obsession~~ passion for the subject matter discussed (and have requested to remain anonymous); and, my late step-grandfather, Jack Flynn, a man who personified the critical thinker.

Also thanks to: the reader who persevered through my initial attempt at fiction; my Friesen Press account manager, Susan Mayo, for her guidance and advice through the publishing process; and, Paul Chefurka (www.paulchefurka.ca) who gave me permission to use his graphs in the story.

Finally, I want to thank the authors whose words I have quoted throughout the book. Their words, along with the voices of many others, have helped me to view the world in a way that is uncomfortable but more realistic. And, by voices I mean other authors, not the voices in my head; they're something altogether different.

www.olduvai.ca

About The Author

Steve Bull lives with his wife and two teenaged daughters in what was once a small town north of Toronto. He has witnessed increasing amounts of limited, fertile farmland disappear as politicians seek the Holy Grail of *progress*: growth. He's more than a little disappointed that decision-makers and policy-leaders, from those in local towns to nation states, are following a path of certain collapse, repeating mistakes that have been made by the leaders of numerous complex societies before them.

Steve sees *the-powers-that-be* ignoring the signs all around them because they believe *this time is different*. And it is different, because this time the collapse will be global in nature.

With a background in archaeology and education, and a goal to inform and entertain, as well as challenge some fundamental beliefs, Steve uses an extension of current events to weave the tale of a group of disparate and desperate people as they encounter the collapse of the economic, social, and political systems around them. Is his story a portent of what our not-too-distant future could look like?

CPSIA information can be obtained
at www.ICGtesting.com
Printed in the USA
FSHW010756060621
82136FS